THESE BOOTS ARE MADE FOR WITCHING

T.M. CROMER

CHAPTER ONE

"You're under arrest."

A high-powered LED flashlight beam blinded her, making it impossible for Payton Hawthorne to see the uniformed officer intent on hauling her to the pokey.

But she recognized the voice. It had haunted her dreams for the last few years.

Dailey Cobb.

Her ex-fiancé and the one that got away.

Or rather, the one she left standing at the altar.

Payton froze in place, unable to speak.

Her best friend and current partner in crime, Rowan Sanderson, had no such problem. "Listen, Officer Knob—"

"Cobb," he ground out.

"You sure?" Rowan squinted like she believed he was lying. "Because you're being a total knob—"

"Ro!" Payton cleared her throat. It was time to take back the reins of this out-of-control sleigh ride. "Right. So, I

know you probably hear this a lot, but it isn't what it looks like."

"You're right," he replied. "I hear it a lot."

He didn't lower the beam as he approached, and she raised a hand to shield her eyes. The unmistakable sound of handcuffs clinking as they cleared their holder was intimidating as hell.

"I'm pretty sure those are the exact words you used when I caught you sneaking out the window on our wedding day," he said coldly. "Now turn around. You're under arrest."

"Lee, please, you don't understand—"

"I don't want to, either. And my name is Officer Cobb to you, Hawthorne."

He moved into the ring of light provided by the overhead street lamp, looking for all the world like an avenging angel as the beam caught and highlighted his close-cropped golden hair.

Payton tamped down the regret.

Dailey Cobb's handsomeness hadn't faded since she initially bolted. If anything, he'd grown hotter. But those steel gray eyes were no longer molten silver when they looked at her. Instead, they were flat, resembling aged concrete in need of a good pressure wash, and except for a burning anger, those once-incredible, sparkling eyes were now dispassionate and bordered on lifeless.

She sensed the simmering rage underneath his cool, collected exterior, and it cut deeply, knowing there was no forgiveness in him. But how much could she expect when she was always in the wrong?

With a worried glance at Rowan, Payton stepped backward and hid her hands behind her.

"You understand that's resisting arrest, don't you?" Dailey asked. "That's going to add more time to your sentence."

Why did he have to sound so gleeful at adding another charge to her B&E?

"Lee—" His thundercloud expression had her correcting her slip. "Uh, Officer Kno—Cobb! Officer *Cobb*... I, uh... that is to say, *we*... we're not breaking the law. This is all a misunderstanding concerning my sister's engagement party." She ended with a sigh and gave him a weak-ass smile. "So there's really no need to arrest us."

"Party? To be clear, you've been partying tonight?"

"Well, ye—er, no! No, not at all." But she had, and she was the worst liar on the planet. A fact he knew well.

"You'll have to take a breathalyzer."

Rowan ran.

With her long, auburn hair flying behind her like the flag of a retreating troop, she took off for the surrounding woods, leaping like a gazelle over half-formed snow drifts. Not once did she check to see if Payton was keeping up.

And damned if Deputy DoRight didn't let her go. Why not? He wasn't concerned with Rowan. His main goal was to make Payton's life a living hell ever since the day she decided to spare him from the misery of marriage to her.

"She always leaves you holding the bag," he said. "You have terrible taste in friends, Hawthorne."

"Her fight-or-flight instincts kicked in. It's the wolf thing. Also, being burned as a witch in a previous life makes her skittish around authority figures."

"Makes sense. Are we doing this the easy way or the hard way?"

She shouldn't have felt the thrill of his words down to her toes, but the low, suggestive way he spoke reminded her of the times they'd spent between the sheets. They'd never had a problem with sex. Their issues had stemmed outside the bedroom.

"It's Elara and Tripp's engagement party, Officer Cobb." Did she see a softening of his expression? She flattened her hand over his uniformed chest. "Will you just overlook this one, er, indiscretion?"

He stared into her beseeching eyes for the longest moment before his gaze dropped to her lips. "What are you proposing?"

Sensing success, she sidled closer. "What do you want?" she asked.

A wicked grin curled his mouth, and she experienced another zing. His voice was friendly, almost teasing, when he asked, "Are you offering me a bribe, Payton Hawthorne?"

"I suppose I am," she replied huskily, caught up in the nostalgia of being close to him again, recalling how wonderful it had felt to be pleasured by a man who loved her.

He lowered his head as if he were about to kiss her, but at the last second, he shifted, lifted a strand of her dark blonde hair to rub between his fingers, and whispered into the shell of her ear. "I'm adding attempting to bribe an officer to your charges."

His tone was so deep and sexy that she didn't at first register what he was saying. Yet the feel of the metal enclosing her wrist snapped her out of the sexual haze he so effortlessly wove.

Damned warlocks!

Payton jerked back, but it was too late. He'd already snapped the cuff in place and secured her opposite wrist within his large, unrelenting grip.

"Please, Lee," she whispered. "Please don't do this. Don't ruin Elara's night."

"I'm not ruining her night. You did that by driving under the influence, breaking and entering a business, resisting arrest, and bribing an officer of the law." His smile was smug, and she wanted to strike him. "Looks like you'll be spending a lot of time behind bars. That can't be easy for someone who prefers to run away rather than deal with her problems."

"What happened with us was more than dealing with a singular problem, and you damned well know it," she retorted.

"Right. You didn't want the commitment of marriage to *me*. The man who once loved you."

The man who once loved you.

Did she hear an emphasis on the word once? She shouldn't still feel a pang whenever she thought of what they had, of what she'd impetuously thrown away. But she did.

"No, I didn't want the constant commitment of being ruled by your *mother*. The mayor of this podunk town," Payton stressed as if he didn't already know how much power his mother held.

Although his brows shot up, he appeared unmoved.

"You already know that, but whatever." She lifted her cuffed arms. "Throw the book at me if it makes you feel like a big man."

"That's the thing, Payton. I haven't felt anything since you disappeared again last year. Not one goddamned thing except anger. And you're going to fix the curse you put on me before you run away this time."

"Curse?" Dumbfounded, she gaped. What the hell was he talking about? "What curse?"

Dailey didn't believe Payton's innocent act regarding the curse for one split second. Last year, she'd stood in that blasted alley, holding her sister's hand, as the magic engulfed him and stole essential emotions from his person. From his peripheral vision, he'd registered Tripp Nightshade's shock and horror as the demigod witnessed their power combined, though he'd tried to hide it.

The demigod's fear resulted from a silly legend surrounding a pair of ridiculous purple boots Elara was wearing. Dailey wasn't positive the blame could be laid on the "fatal footwear," as Tripp had referred to those shoes, or whether the women unknowingly unleashed their own brand of hell on him, but he wanted whatever witchcraft they'd used neutralized.

Immediately.

"Look, I get you're the queen of playing people and excel at games, but I'm over you and all of this." Her mouth dropped open, and the wounded expression she affected left him cold. "I'll drop the charges and release you if you reverse the evil mojo."

"Lee—"

He scowled at her wheedling tone and crossed his arms.

"Uh, I mean, Officer Cobb,"—she cleared her throat—"I'm honestly clueless about your supposed curse."

Fury was one of the few remaining emotions he felt, and

though he should be grateful to feel anything at all, it annoyed him to have anger overrule his peace or happiness. Not that he'd experienced anything resembling glitter and roses after she'd left him standing at the altar—with his proverbial dick in hand—as she Houdini'd it out of a bedroom window.

The outrage building inside him cemented his half-baked decision to abduct and hold her hostage until she agreed to reverse the spell. Wordlessly, he led her to his Tahoe, opened the back door, and placed a hand atop her blonde head, guiding her into the bench seat.

"Payton Hawthorne, you're under arrest. You have the right to remain silent—not that you will—"

"Fuck off! This is spiteful and childish, even for a Cobb!" Her reddening face scrunched as if she fought against shedding the welling tears in her wide aquamarine eyes.

The sight should've moved him—actually would've once—but the black hole of nothingness inside ate whatever emotional response he might've had.

"Spiteful? Childish?" He snorted and rested his elbow on the roof. "Childish is running away from the man you supposedly love without bothering to have an adult conversation and fix what you perceive to be wrong. Childish is leaving him to face a congregation of friends and family to tell them his bride didn't care enough to stick. And cursing a man to feel nothing for you or anyone else for an entire year?" He leaned in. "That, my darling Payton, is *spiteful*. This"—he gestured between them—"yeah, it may be a little payback, but it's not like I can take enjoyment from it."

"Then what is it? Why not 'have an adult conversation and fix what you perceive to be wrong?'" she sneered.

"Good question," he muttered. One for which he didn't have an answer. "Anything you say can and will be used against you in a court of law—"

"Fucking asshole!" she shouted, kicking at him.

"Assaulting an officer is illegal, too," he reminded her as he skillfully dodged her heel. "You have a right to an attorney. If you cannot afford an attorney, one will be appointed for you."

Fury had replaced her initial shock and upset. Her lips were compressed so tightly they were colorless and outlined in white. If she weren't a witch with healing abilities, he might consider her blood pressure and the potential for a stroke.

"Do you understand these rights as I've said them to you?" he asked.

Chin lifted high, Payton gave one short nod before averting her face in dismissal. Damned if she didn't appear heartbreakingly fragile.

Tingling started in his chest as if his soul were sparking back to life. It fizzled as if someone had flipped on a light, only to turn it off mid-flip of the switch. Frowning, he closed the door and went to retrieve her personal items. After locking up her car, he cast a quick location charm and scanned the woods beyond the road. Dailey immediately spotted a heat signature behind a tree about fifty yards out.

"You've not seen anything, Rowan Sanderson, or I'll haul your ass in for the B&E, too, got it?" he called.

Her growled "fuck off" echoed through the trees.

Once, he'd have laughed at her cheeky response, but not tonight.

"Remember what I said and who runs this town."

She stepped from her hiding spot, hands on her hips. "Did you ever consider that arrogant attitude is why she left you, you fucking tool?"

He had.

Many times.

But only because Elara had been forthcoming with why Payton had run away: his dismissal of her fears concerning his mother's managing ways. Yet, how was one supposed to completely alienate their family or overhaul their personality?

He'd made allowance after allowance for his fiancée's wild side. Initially, he'd been worried a small part of him was relieved when she left despite his crushing pain. But as time went on, his hurt grew. There had been plenty of opportunities for her to tell him she was experiencing second thoughts. Waiting until their wedding day? Yeah, that was just fucking cold.

Ignoring Rowan, he turned on his heel and stalked back to his cruiser. He swore under his breath when he spotted the handcuffs dangling from the door handle and the empty backseat. For the briefest moment, he'd forgotten she possessed an uncanny ability to slip her bindings. It was definitely something he should've remembered, considering how they'd liked to kink things up in the bedroom.

The tingling started again, and he surprised himself when he laughed.

"Game on, Hawthorne!" he called out, knowing damned well she'd hear him. "Game on."

CHAPTER TWO

Dailey found it challenging to believe Payton wasn't aware of the curse despite her protests. The worst part was being ordered by Elara to go away and feeling like he had no control over his actions. He'd been nothing more than a marionette at the end of her puppet-master strings. That, he couldn't forgive.

His mother had been correct about one thing: the Hawthornes were no good.

Not because they'd come from the "wrong side of the tracks," as she so often said, but because they were selfish, uncaring about anyone else.

After pocketing Payton's keys and retrieving his cuffs, Dailey climbed into his cruiser and sped off. Yes, he could circle back, and likely should, but for now, he'd let her go. It wasn't as if Witchmere was a bustling metropolis, making it difficult to find a criminal.

And his intent wasn't to take her to jail.

No, when he found her again, he would take her to his cabin. There, they'd have a long-overdue discussion about her stunted emotional growth and inability to love. Then, once he'd read her the riot act and given her time to process the deep shit she was in, he'd offer an out: in exchange for removing the hex, she was free to depart his town and never return.

He paused, waiting for the familiar pang he'd always experienced whenever he thought of her leaving forever.

Nothing.

Good.

Maybe the curse wasn't so terrible after all.

An unexpected image of her on their last night together formed in his mind. She'd been troubled when he arrived home, but quickly masked it with a cheerful façade. If he'd pressed harder instead of letting her convince him it was no big deal, they might still be together.

But did he want a woman who hated everything about him? One who mocked what he stood for? She was a virtual child in a pornstar's body, never forced to grow up. In fairness, her parents had deserted her at a formative age. But Elara managed to do just fine, aside from her impulsive spellcasting and her random dodging into alleys to avoid people. Although he'd considered using her tactic a time or two.

Throughout the evening, Dailey contemplated his next move.

Coldly.

Calculatingly.

He could stake out Elara's old apartment on the off chance Payton hadn't returned to the engagement party. Or perhaps he'd wake her at the ass-crack of dawn when she was suffering the hangover from hell.

He refused to question why he didn't simply confront Elara instead of Payton. Maybe because his ex-fiancée's betrayal was much more personal, considering everything they'd shared.

By the Gods, he'd loved her. Obsessively, to his mother's way of thinking and probably Payton's, too. Had he unintentionally smothered her in his need to keep her close? If he were being honest with himself, he'd have to admit it was probable. His childhood had been void of baser emotions, mainly because Mother found outbursts and spontaneity distasteful. No child of *hers* would become a needy hooligan ruled by their feelings—her words, not his. Mayor Mary-Alice Cobb had an image to uphold, and she'd never let her children forget it.

Perhaps his sister, Sloane, had the right idea when she escaped. Although the way she'd done it wasn't the wisest. Marrying Bradford, the "Bougie Biscuit" as she called him, had been an epic mistake on her part. It seemed neither Dailey nor his sister possessed the best taste when selecting life partners. In Sloane's case, their mother adored Bradford and despised her daughter. In Dailey's, she loathed Payton and doted on him, much to his embarrassment and detriment. Their brother, Harrison, had mostly flown under the radar and seemed to be the only well-adjusted of the three. But then again, he'd chosen psychology as a major. Maybe he'd gained insight into how to survive their domineering parent.

"Goddamn it," he muttered.

Another tingle coursed through him, and he frowned.

Either he was experiencing a magical disruption, or his nerve endings were on the fritz.

His radio crackled.

"Chief?"

Dailey sighed. Why the hell did he feel older than his forty-two years? It didn't bode well for him that warlocks lived longer than the average bear.

"Yeah, Junior, what is it?" he asked tiredly.

"Chief, we have a problem."

When no further explanation followed, he counted to ten. "It would be helpful if you spit it out, kid."

"Oh, yeah, right."

Dailey pressed his thumb between his brows and exhaled heavily.

Junior Jenkins was twenty-one and still green. The guy believed everything was an emergency when it wasn't, could barely reason his way out of a paper bag, and didn't understand nuances like sarcasm. If Dailey hadn't promised the kid's mom he'd look after him, he'd have cut him loose five minutes after Junior started his internship.

"Are you going to tell me anytime tonight, Junior, or am I supposed to guess?"

"Sorry, sir. But Payton—"

"I'll be right there." Dailey did a sharp U-turn in the center of town and headed for the station. Once there, he took the steps two at a time and jerked the door open, stopping short when he saw Tripp Nightshade.

He was leaning back in Dailey's chair with his feet on the desk. Dressed in all his finery with black, shoulder-length hair and a chiseled jawline that the faces of Mount Rushmore would envy, the demigod appeared out of place but commanding despite the fact.

Fuck.

Tripp's black brow lifted in amusement. "Expecting someone else?"

"What do you want, Nightshade?" Dailey asked evenly, keeping it together and refusing to rise to the bait.

"Payton's keys, for a start."

"Sorry, but she'll have to pick those up herself." He crossed his arms, making it clear he wasn't budging.

"Junior, find something else to do," Tripp said, with a casual flick of his hand in the young man's direction.

With eyes glazed over, Junior obediently walked away like a spell-snatched sheep.

"I'd appreciate it if you and your new fiancée would stop throwing out the mind-altering incantations. They're not beads at a Mardi Gras parade." Dailey dropped his arms and stalked forward. "Your lack of consequence is a real issue, Nightshade."

"Elara didn't understand the power those boots contained, Cobb. Hermes has indicated your curse will wear off when the timing is right."

Dailey shoved Tripp's designer-clad feet off his desk. "What the hell is that supposed to mean, 'when the timing is right?' I want it gone *now*."

As if on cue, Hermes strolled through the double doors. "It's not within his ability, Constable Curseday. It was the result of Titan magic mixed with Trickster magic. Unbreakable until it plays out."

Hermes bore a striking resemblance to his cousin, Tripp, but where Nightshade's eyes were obsidian and cool, the Trickster's were a bold emerald and contained a perpetual devilish twinkle, indicating he was rarely serious.

"Bullshit." Dailey didn't believe for one second that the god couldn't reverse the curse. The asshole simply didn't want to.

Hermes grinned, and he never wanted to taser a person more.

"I'm going to bring Payton in, and when I do, the three of you will work out how to remove whatever fuckery has numbed my emotions. Got it?"

With narrowed eyes, the Trickster studied him. "I'm not certain what difference it makes whether your feelings were numbed or not. You've clearly been emotionally stunted since birth."

Because it was too close to the truth, Dailey didn't respond. Only with Payton had he felt alive, and there were days he missed the sensation. Missed the laughter. What he didn't miss was the pain of their arguments or the disappointment he experienced whenever she was unhappy. And he certainly didn't want to relive the soul-crushing agony of her running away on their wedding day.

"Clear out. I have work to do." And a brother to call. Perhaps Harrison, with all his therapeutic wisdom, could coach him on how to cope. Dailey's liver wasn't happy with his drinking himself into a whiskey-induced coma every night.

Tripp climbed to his feet, pausing beside him on his way to the exit. "Consider this, Cobb. Payton had nothing to do with your curse. She didn't know Elara's amped-up spell took hold until tonight." He gave Dailey's shoulder a quick squeeze. "The woman I've come to know would never do anything to hurt you."

The tingling started again, and with its return, Dailey's chest ached.

"That's rich, and a damned lie," he snapped. "She ripped my fucking heart out when she turned tail and ran, not caring about the destruction she left in her wake. If you believe she wouldn't do it again, you're a fool."

Although he frowned, Tripp didn't reply right away. Eventually, he said, "I'm sorry you suffered, Dailey. But it was years ago."

"Time may weather the stone, but the carvings remain, Nightshade. Remember that." He turned away, desperate to escape their oppressive power lingering in the air.

And maybe a small part of him understood how overwhelming it had been for Payton to deal with two powerful beings in one room when she didn't have magic of her own.

It was worth considering.

"Get Junior back on duty."

CHAPTER THREE

Payton nearly jumped out of her skin when the door slammed shut, but she'd be damned if she would check to see who'd just stormed into the apartment. Cowardly, yes, but with her luck, Dailey had found her and was ready to drag her butt to the pokey. She'd barely managed to escape without him catching her the first time.

"You here?" Rowan called.

Dropping her shoulders and shrugging off her disappointment at her visitor not being the man she loved, Payton stormed out of the bedroom and into the living room.

"Some friend you are!" she yelled. "You left me at the first sign of trouble."

"I can't help it. It's my wolfy fight-or-flight instincts."

"That's pretty much what I said to Lee," Payton said with a sour look.

"Yeah, and being burned—"

She held up a hand. "I told him that, too."

Rowan's brows shot up. "What did he say?"

"That I have terrible taste in friends."

She laughed. Therein lay Rowan's true beauty. Not only was she the perfect package on the outside, but when her amusement took hold, she was breathtaking. It still astonished Payton whenever she thought about how Harrison Cobb was completely oblivious to her friend's charms.

Payton rolled her eyes as she pushed past her to lock the door. Not that it mattered. If Dailey decided to storm the castle, so to speak, he'd simply flick a finger and unlock the deadbolt.

Right as she was about to give her bestie a firm dressing down, a knock sounded, causing them to freeze. Rowan's green eyes flew wide, and it wasn't hard to guess her F&F instincts were warring again.

"Stay calm," Payton hissed. She peered through the peephole and, seeing no one but a deliveryman, exhaled her relief. "It's just a package."

The door was halfway open when Rowan posed a terrifying question. "What company delivers at midnight?"

"Motherfuck—"

The guy pushed into the room, and the glamour fell away, revealing Dailey.

The glass sliding door whooshed open behind her, but Payton didn't need to look to know Rowan had bailed again.

"That bitch," she muttered.

Dailey snorted. "It's not like she could save you, and she knew it."

"A little moral support would be nice." Payton plopped down on the chair and reached for the footwear she'd kicked off ten minutes before. "Let me get these on, and I'll go peacefully this time."

"Relax. I'm off duty and tired as hell. We'll take this up again in the morning." He shut the door on the way to the kitchen. "What do you have to eat?"

After she managed to pull her jaw off the floor, she shook her head. "I'm not sure. Elara stocked the fridge today, but I only just got here before her party. I didn't have time to explore." She toed her shoe off, beyond thrilled she didn't need to wear heels to jail. Her feet were already killing her from all the dancing earlier. Padding to the counter, she climbed onto a stool and tucked her chin in hand.

"Why are you being nice? If you didn't come to arrest me, what is the point of showing up this late?"

Dailey peered around the refrigerator door, eyebrows almost to his hairline. "You think I'm being nice?"

"For you. Lately."

"Fair." He set eggs, cheese, a slew of vegetables, and butter on the counter. "Omelet?"

"No." Waving him off, she stumbled to the pantry. "I'm good with chips."

"Your diet is as horrific as your friends, Pay."

"Not much has changed in the last few years." She paused, snack halfway to her mouth. "I'm sorry, Lee, I didn't—"

"Don't call me that," he snapped.

"You're going to insist on Officer Knob—er, *Cobb*?"

"No. Dailey works well enough," he said grudgingly as he dumped a teaspoon of butter into a pan.

She couldn't say she didn't get it. When he called her

"Pay," her heart had flipped, and that old gooey feeling had filled her chest. Nicknames were off the table if they wanted any semblance of friendship moving forward.

"I'll ask again. What is the point of showing up here?" she asked softly.

"I had a plan until Tripp and Hermes shot it to hell."

Payton didn't love the way his mouth tightened with disappointment. Throughout their entire relationship, Dailey always scheduled out his days, weeks, and hell, even his months. If his newest scheme had gone to ruin, he'd be scrambling to right it or come up with a new one.

Hunger forgotten, she rolled the top of the bag and shoved it back onto the pantry shelf. "Dare I ask what 'it' was?"

He glanced up from chopping a pepper. "It?"

"The plan," she replied.

"No," he said succinctly.

"Dailey."

"Drop it. All I want is to eat my omelet in peace."

Hands on hips and glare in full force, she snapped, "Then maybe you shouldn't have come here."

He turned off the burner and shoved the pan toward the back of the stovetop.

"Fine," he replied. "You want to argue, let's argue."

The fine lines around his eyes seemed deeper, and his lips were pinched, as if he was really fighting fatigue. Payton felt like a raging bitch. Her throat grew tight as they stared at one another.

How in the hell would she ever walk away from him a second time? But it wasn't like she had a choice, right? It wasn't as if he were there to patch things up by promising the moon and stars, along with kicking his mother to the curb.

"I'm sorry," she croaked. And she wasn't sure what she was apologizing for: running away or ruining his meal. Likely both.

Dailey rounded the counter to stand before her, and the force of his presence made the room too small.

"You were the only peace I had in Witchmere. Is it so odd I'd seek your company when I'm feeling unsettled today?" he asked.

"Yes. Not four hours ago, you hated me and wanted to arrest me."

His disturbing gaze dropped to her lips, and he stared as if he were contemplating kissing her.

"True." He nodded slowly, as if just remembering the fact. "Though I didn't hate you. I was angry, which seems to be my default setting these days." He locked gazes with her. "But I discovered something else in the interim."

"What's that?"

"You made me laugh when I believed I couldn't." He frowned. "When I'm around you, I experience a tingling, as if my soul is trying to wake up again," he confessed.

"I've always had that," she replied softly, cupping his jaw.

For a brief instant, he closed his eyes and allowed the touch, rolling his cheek into her palm. But he quickly woke from whatever enchantment they'd been weaving. Stepping back, he broke the contact.

"Yeah, well…" He cleared his throat.

Because she missed the feel of him, she stepped forward and placed her palm against his chest.

"Why do you stay in Witchmere if it causes you unrest?"

"Where else would I go?" he asked, turning away to finish whipping the eggs.

"Literally anywhere."

"You mean run away? Like you?" Tone stiff and shoulders rigid, he shot her a scathing glance.

"You're never going to forgive me, are you?" The ache in her chest was so acute, she couldn't catch her breath. It couldn't hurt worse if he plunged a blade into her heart.

Dailey hung his head, and his sigh was soul weary.

"I don't know, Pay. I honestly don't know." When he met her tearful gaze, his expression softened. "Maybe. One day."

Any forgiveness at all was more than she deserved.

She nodded and hip-checked him to take over his meal.

"Go sit down, Dailey. Rest your feet, and I'll make this."

"It's not going to get you out of trouble. You were drinking and driving."

"Prove it. Anything I may have consumed—and I'm not admitting to shit without a lawyer present—is out of my system." Thank you, high metabolism!

His grin flashed, almost taking her out at the knees. "Same ol' Payton. You'll fight authority until your dying day."

"Probably. Now go. I can't concentrate with you this close." She could've bitten her fucking tongue off when his smile widened.

Dailey kicked off his work boots and settled on the couch, propping his feet on the coffee table. Grabbing one of the decorative pillows, he tucked it behind his head and closed his eyes. His earlier dreams had all consisted of him coming home to a smiling Payton and a delicious home-cooked or conjured meal. The idea was to rest until he got a second wind, then make love to her all night.

But his vision of the perfect life had been dashed the day she'd bolted.

Recalling better times, he drifted to sleep.

"Dailey." Her voice floated to him on a wave of perfume —gardenias and something wild, totally Payton.

Wrapped in a haze of desire and longing, he lifted his lids. And there she was, apron around her waist, plate in hand, soft smile on display. His perfect mate.

"You fell asleep," she said.

She hadn't left him?

"It was all a nightmare?" he asked, bleary-eyed and feeling half-drugged.

"What?"

Her confusion cleared his cobwebs, and he shook his head, reaching for the dish she offered.

"Yeah, sorry," he muttered, vastly disappointed this was his reality. Clearly he'd been haunted by the ghost of Christmas past.

"I'll leave you in peace to eat your omelet."

"Stay," he urged, latching on to her wrist.

She appeared shocked that he'd voluntarily touched her. Embarrassment was a new emotion, but it sent heat up his throat and into his cheeks.

"Sorry."

"No, it's cool." She sat beside him, hugging a pillow as she curled her legs beneath her. And damned if she didn't look like a seductive goddess.

But he supposed she was. Or as close to it as possible.

Last Christmas, it came out that she and Elara were of Titan descent. The fact explained so much: her not-so-subtle allure, his undying attraction to her even when he wanted to murder her, and his inability to eradicate her from his mind.

"Have your abilities blossomed since your parents removed their binding spell?" he asked, curious despite himself. He shoveled in a forkful, and when Payton opened her mouth to reply, Dailey cut her off with an appreciative groan. "Mm, this is incredible. When did you learn to cook like this?"

"It's no different than any omelet I've made for you. You're the one who prepped the ingredients," she said with a light laugh.

"No, you did something different," he insisted, inhaling another bite.

"Cross my heart, I didn't." She followed her words with action.

He frowned down at his food. "Pay—"

"Your food is untouched by magic, Dailey," she said tightly. Tossing the pillow down, she rose. "I wouldn't do that to you."

Appetite gone, he scraped his plate and prepared to clean the kitchen, only to realize she already had. Feeling like ten kinds of fool, he sought her out.

Sitting alone in the center of the large bed, she appeared lost.

"I'm sorry it seemed like I was accusing you of anything sketchy, Payton. I guess I forgot how good your cooking is." He cast her a half smile. "I still think you should've gone into business with Britney Sanderson. Her management skills and your magic in the kitchen…" He blew a chef's kiss. "Dream team."

Her ghost of a return smile was melancholy. "Yes. I missed a golden opportunity. Good night, Dailey."

As far as hints went, hers had all the subtlety of a sledgehammer.

"We need to talk," he began.

"Not tonight." Her steely tone said she wouldn't relent. With an arched brow and an uncaring shrug, she asked, "When are you on duty again?"

"Seven."

She gasped and glanced at her smartwatch. "In the morning? Dailey! You're not allowing yourself enough downtime between shifts."

His irritation spiked. The fault was hers. He'd rather work himself into a stupor than have free time to recall what they'd had. And he sure as shit hadn't been able to move on after her stunt in the alleyway. Resolve shifted back into place, and he set his jaw.

"Be at the station as soon as you've had your morning coffee, Hawthorne."

Shit. Wrong thing for him to say. Her narrow-eyed glare said it would happen when a blizzard happened in hell, and Dailey fought the urge to chuckle.

Again with the amusement! What was happening? Was the curse running its course like Hermes and Tripp suggested?

If that were the case, he'd be sad. He'd yet to enact his revenge.

Speaking of…

His lips curled, and placing one knee on the mattress, he caged her between his arms.

Her breath hitched along with something in his chest.

"I'll tell you what. You—" he began.

She palmed his face and shoved. "Get out, tool."

"You don't even know what I was going to say," he protested with a laugh.

"I can damn well guess, and I don't bargain with sex." With her arms crossed and her chin jutted skyward, she presented a challenge. Dailey loved nothing more than a daring woman.

"Really? I could swear you attempted to bribe an officer of the law earlier tonight." He tapped his chin like he was attempting to recall. "As a matter of fact, it's one of the charges I'll be leveling against you. For the record, our entire exchange was caught on my body cam."

"I hate you." Like a thwarted child, she kicked out.

He evaded the blow, dancing away from the bed. The tingling was back, and his cells had never felt more alive despite his lack of sleep.

"See you tomorrow, jailbird." With a wink, he turned to go.

"Not if I see you first."

Pausing in the doorway, he met her furious gaze. "You're better than such an overused cliché, Wildfire."

She sputtered, but thankfully in her anger missed him calling her by his pet name.

What in the blue blazes had come over him tonight? Not once, but twice. First arriving here, needing to see her at the end of a trying day, and second calling her the nickname he reserved for their steamiest nights.

She jumped up and stalked his way.

"Fine. How about the next time you see me, it will be with my lawyer present, Officer *Knob*? Does that pack enough snark for you?"

Dailey did his damnedest not to laugh, going so far as to bite the inside of his cheek.

"Better, but still not your best," he taunted.

"Then let's go with this one. If you think you'll ever get the last word, you're dumber than your mother's brainless Pomeranian, Officer Knob," she replied smugly, going so far as to slam the door in his face.

His blood heated, but not with the standard anger he'd felt over the previous year. No, his body was primed and ready for a different game.

Whistling a jaunty tune, he teleported to his house. Tomorrow would be soon enough to retrieve his cruiser.

CHAPTER FOUR

Banging woke Payton, and she wished Dailey Cobb straight to perdition. He had to know he'd wormed his way into her thoughts and that she'd stayed up well past a sane person's bedtime reliving the night's events. Was it too much to ask for a damned break?

She twisted her wrist to check the time. With a few choice swearwords, she removed her smartwatch and dropped it onto the charger. Sure, she could've given it a boost, but batteries and magic didn't always play nice.

The banging resumed, and Payton was fully prepared to eviscerate whoever dared knock again. With a growl, she stomped into the foyer and yanked open the door. She blinked down at the festively decorated box, then leaned into the hallway to check both directions. From around the corner, the elevator dinged, but she'd be damned if she gave chase.

Caffeine first, present second, dealing with Dailey third.

Or preferably never.

Never would be good.

She scooched the box inside with her foot, slammed the door, then headed for the kitchen. Centered on her spotless counter was a large to-go cup with a sticky note attached.

You have until 11 a.m. — D.

Payton crumpled the paper and removed the lid from what she suspected was the perfectly flavored coffee. One sip confirmed that the temperature and taste were spot on, and she sighed her appreciation.

Dailey's thoughtfulness was suspect. Was he trying to soften her only to lay down the hammer later? Why? What would be the point when she was already expecting the worst? Perhaps it was to ensure she showed up for her punishment.

Frowning, she smoothed the note flat. At some point this morning, he'd left her this gift, likely spelling it to stay hot. Dailey wouldn't have forgotten her night-owl tendencies. He never forgot any of her preferences. Once learned, he'd locked them in and made sure to deliver.

Payton had missed his special brand of consideration. Most lovers were pleasure-focused and transactional. Not him, though. He had always paid close attention.

Swallowing past the lump in her throat wasn't easy, but she managed to consume the required amount of caffeine to function. Awake enough to investigate the delivery, she retrieved the box from the foyer. When she peeled off the wrapping paper and lifted the lid, she gasped. Inside were the most stunning boots she'd ever seen.

Deep burgundy velvet, so rich it should be illegal, hugged a shape designed to ruin a woman for all other footwear. Hundreds of tiny crystals caught the light and threw it right back in glittering defiance. The kind of sparkle that said, "I dare you not to look."

She lifted one boot out, already halfway in love, and turned it in her hands. The lace-up front oozed vintage seduction, with velvety ribbon threaded through polished eyelets. But it was the heel that did her in—sleek, silver, and sharp enough to stab a mofo through the heart.

Of course, Dailey remembered her tastes: dramatic on the gooey side of decadent.

Dailey Cobb didn't merely give a gift. Apparently, he issued a declaration, and this one screamed, "I still know you, Payton. I still want you." Although she'd never entered a relationship for financial gain, she certainly never objected to a man spoiling her. These boots were intended to appeal to her inner glam girl, and they fit perfectly beside the spectacular Christmas presents he'd given her when they were a couple.

"Oh, you thoughtful sonofabitch," she whispered, warmth filling her cold, hollowed-out heart.

She kissed the bedazzled tip of the boot and nestled it back into the tissue. After a shower and a little strategic makeup, she intended to put those babies on and meet Dailey at the assigned time. Being prompt was the least she could do.

Yet as she stepped under the steamy waterfall, she considered the pitfalls associated with beginning again. Would he tell his mother to butt out this time? Payton found it hard to believe Mary-Alice Cobb would let him run his own life, illustrious Chief of Police of Witchmere or not.

With a sigh, she dried off, closed her eyes, and conjured the perfect outfit: a long-sleeved, body-skimming black knit sweater dress that hit mid-thigh. It hugged her curves and was toasty enough for the chilly December morning.

After checking her reflection, she snapped her fingers to dip the neckline and flash a teasing amount of collarbone. One wave of her hand opened her accessory drawer. Yes, the velvet burgundy choker would match perfectly. She'd add her favorite dagger pendant with the winking blood-red ruby.

Next, she stepped into her new glittery boots. The fit was exceptional, and once again, Payton credited Dailey with keen observation skills. She strode back and forth across the living room, testing the comfort, surprised they felt as good as they did.

"Perfect," she sighed.

One by one, the crystals lit, pulsing with a breathtaking pink glow.

The tingling in her lower extremities was an "oh shit" moment, and a heat wave swept upward to her core, firing her up in ways all too similar to her wanton nights with Dailey. The next surge tightened her stomach, and sweat broke out at her temples.

Then she knew.

"Hermes! You asshole!" she swore. "Why didn't I put two and two together the instant I saw these damned boots?"

"Perhaps because they're a different color and style, suited specifically for you?" replied a deeply amused voice.

She spun toward the sliding porch door and found the Divine Trickster himself.

"Why?" she cried. "Didn't they cause enough havoc when Elara wore them? The entire town was almost destroyed by a volcano, for fuck's sake!"

"That's only because Enguerrand was a stubborn fool. It's not likely to happen again." Hermes shrugged one deliciously muscled shoulder as if it didn't matter one way or the other.

He was such an arrogant, cagey bastard.

"Not likely? But it *could?*" she asked, sitting down, prepared to rip the cursed boots from her feet.

"Those won't come off until their mission is completed, love. Don't waste your time trying."

Dismay built into a feeling remarkably similar to full-blown panic, and worked its way toward her spasming throat.

"What are they going to make me do?" she croaked in horror.

Hermes frowned. His emerald eyes were dark with concern when he squatted before her.

"Just breathe, Payton. It will all work out. I promise."

"You can't promise anything. If I recall correctly, and I always do, these fucking things take on a life of their own, *outside* of your ability to control them. How the hell are you going to fix it when things go sideways?"

In the distance, the town clock rang the first of eleven times.

"Crap! I have to go. Dailey's expecting me. If I'm late..." She didn't care to think what he'd do if she didn't show at the designated time, especially considering he wasn't the one gifting her boots.

She deflated.

They weren't from him. Which meant all the old love she attributed to him meant nothing.

Last night's events loomed in her mind, and a fresh new fear struck. Did he intend to arrest her? Was it too late to leave Witchmere for good?

"Yes," Hermes said, making Payton realize she'd spoken aloud. "You have to see the spell to completion."

"Goddess, I hate everyone," she muttered.

She wasn't showing.

Dailey couldn't say he was surprised. Payton was the queen of disappearing acts. But the profound disappointment he experienced was more than he'd felt in a great while, with most of it directed at himself for his ridiculous assumption that she'd meet him.

Feeling ninety, he shoved back his chair and stood.

The outer office buzzed with commotion a second before his door burst open.

And there she was.

A blonde goddess in a black dress with sparkling boots. Her cheeks were flushed, and her eyes were frantic as they locked on him.

"I fully intended to be on time, but Hermes..."

Dailey didn't hear the rest. His mind immediately went to what she didn't say.

Hermes.

The gorgeous fucker who could have anyone he wanted

with a crook of his perfectly formed finger. And he'd probably crooked it at *her*.

He scowled as Payton wrung her hands.

"Lee—er, Dailey?"

Jumping up, he stalked over, tugged her the rest of the
way into his office, and slammed the door. After drawing
the blinds, he faced her. Her lush mouth, glossed a rich
burgundy to match her choker and boots, hung open. They
were lips that begged to be kissed, and suddenly, it was all he
could think about.

"Goddammit," he muttered.

One second, he was sane, and the next, he wasn't. Daily
closed the distance, cradling her face and locking onto the
mesmerizing object of his desire.

"Do you want this as much as I do?" he asked hoarsely.

"This?" Her breathiness hit him low and hard.

"Yes, Wildfire. *This.*" He ran a thumb over her lower lip.

Her eyes flew wide, and she rapidly blinked before
focusing on his mouth. She'd barely finished her nod before
he was kissing her as if he wouldn't survive another day
without tasting her unique spiciness. As if a world of lonely
tomorrows wouldn't exist if he could just evoke an
answering response from her.

And saints above, he did.

She knocked one of his hands away to make room for
her arm around his neck.

Dailey welcomed the freedom so he could grip behind
her knee and hike one long, tantalizing leg around his hip.

Her deep-throated moan nearly did him in. He'd just
lifted an arm, prepared to sweep the surface of his desk,
when someone knocked.

"Uh, Chief?"

Fucking, Junior! Dailey was seriously beginning to despise that kid.

Pulling away, he sighed and exchanged a *What the fuck just possessed us?* look with Payton.

"Chief? Everything okay in there?" Junior called with another rap on the door.

She did an awkward dance, tapping the hand still gripping her thigh as a signal to release her, before she rubbed her thumb across his mouth.

"Lip gloss," she said in answer to his questioning frown.

"Thanks." Raising his voice, Dailey called out, "If it isn't urgent, Junior, I need five minutes." The delay might not kill his erection, but it afforded him time to hide behind his desk.

"Yessir."

After the footsteps faded, he blew out a breath. "Look, I'm sorry. I'm not sure what came over me."

"I have a good idea," she muttered as she sank into the visitor chair.

Oddly, he felt the urge to grin. "You do? Care to explain it to me?"

"I'm not sure you'd believe me if I did."

Her deflated expression bothered him and sent him to his knees in front of her.

With a light brush of his fingers over her flushed cheek, he asked, "What is it, Pay?"

"Hermes."

"There's that fucking name again," He muttered, dropping his arm to stand. "Are you involved with him? Is that why you were late? Why you're upset that I kissed you?"

"What? No! God, Lee. You know me better than that!"

"I thought I did." He crossed to the wall of windows and stared down at the bustling street below. It belatedly occurred to him that the holiday was almost upon them. Yet another one without someone to share it with. "Turns out I didn't, though, did I?" he asked softly.

She joined him, and for a long while, neither spoke.

"You know me better than anyone in my entire life ever has," she said. Glancing up, she added, "Elara and Rowan included."

Dailey scoffed. "That's not saying much."

Hurt flashed across her face.

"Shit, Pay, I didn't mean it to be unkind." But maybe he did. Maybe he'd turned into a bitter bastard who made digs at another's expense. And if so, he didn't like who he'd become. "I'm sorry."

She didn't acknowledge his apology. "Earlier, I was only late because I thought you sent me these boots."

He followed her finger point and noticed her sparkly new footwear.

"Hot, but I didn't send them. I only left coffee and a note," he replied wryly.

"I know." With a roll of her eyes, she looked out over Witchmere's main thoroughfare. Did she see the decorations and, like him, remember happier times?

"They were a gift from the Divine Trickster," she stated woodenly, bringing him back to the conversation. "Apparently, I'm next on his list to terrorize with his fucking magical boots."

His stomach dropped. Sure, he hadn't truly attributed his curse to Elara's choice in shoes, but if those things *were* evil incarnate, as Tripp liked to say, Dailey would prefer they were at the bottom of an ocean and not on Payton's feet.

"Take them off right now!" he ordered, cringing at how autocratic he sounded. His authoritative arrogance would have her doing the exact opposite.

Yet she surprised him. Although her mouth tightened, she didn't read him the riot act as one might expect. Instead saying, "I tried. I'm stuck with them until I've done whatever it is they want."

"Fuck."

"Yeah, my thoughts exactly."

CHAPTER FIVE

"There must be a way to remove them, Pay," Dailey was saying.

But Payton had tried. She'd sweated through ten precious minutes this morning trying to snip the laces, cut the leather, and yank the boots off. The damned things were impenetrable.

"Anyway, that's why I was late, Dailey. I'd put them on, cussed Hermes out the instant the magic activated, then took everything short of a blowtorch to these shoes, before finally teleporting here."

"Considering the circumstances, I'll let your tardiness slide."

She snorted. "You're so generous."

He frowned as if her sarcasm bothered him, when in fact, she knew he was as impervious as the damned boots.

"What is this grand punishment you have planned for me?" she asked tiredly, feeling a hundred years old.

"If they are enchanted, what is it they do?" he asked in return, ignoring her question.

"I don't know," she said, crossing to the visitor chair. "From what Elara told me last year, they were designed to help her and Tripp connect, feeding their love for one another." Payton avoided eye contact as she said, "I'm not sure what they are meant to do for me, though, and I didn't have time to wait for an explanation from that asshole."

"Then let's go find him and see what he'll reveal." Dailey circled the desk, shrugged into his coat, and drew a beanie on over his thick blond hair. He held out his hand. "Ready?"

"You should've been a detective instead of a chief," she blurted.

His dark-blond brows shot up as if waiting for her to elaborate.

So she did. "You come to life when there's a mystery to solve, Lee."

The left side of his mouth kicked up. "You said I know you better than anyone, but the reverse is true, Wildfire. There's always been a part of you I could never reach. Despite that, I'd opened up to you in ways I never had with anyone else." He sobered. "You picked up on my love of mystery and saw through me. Always."

"I loved every aspect of our lives together," she said with a catch in her voice. "Just not your mother steering our future."

"We could've worked that out if you'd just stayed."

"No, Dailey. Because you wouldn't listen. My staying was never going to solve a problem you couldn't see."

He approached her and tilted up her chin to meet his

searching gaze. "Maybe you're right. Maybe we were always destined to fail."

Her blood ran cold.

Yeah, it wasn't what she'd expected him to say, nor was the dismissive shrug one she'd have believed him capable of.

"Let's find Hermes before his games can cause any more damage," he said.

He opened the door, and there, on the other side, was the God himself. Sprawled sideways in a wooden visitor's chair, with one long leg draped over the arm, he examined his perfectly buffed nails, as if bored at being made to wait.

When he glanced up, the impact of his sparkling eyes, so filled with humor, wrecked the careless image he portrayed.

"Ah! Just the couple I was looking for," he said, springing to his feet. "I thought I'd give you the ground rules before things get out of hand, like with Elara and Enguerrand's little dance."

Nerves got the better of Payton, and her belly churned.

"What do you mean, ground rules? And what dance are we talking about here, asshole? Because I didn't sign up for this shit," she demanded.

Hermes's mouth dipped in an exaggerated grimace, but the laughter never left his eyes. "Is she always so… *salty* in the mornings? I'll admit it's a little off-putting. Why, just today, as she was dressing, she—"

Dailey's low, furious growl raised the hair on her neck, and the next moment, he had Hermes by the throat pinned to the wall.

"Oh, leave off, Cowboy," the Trickster drawled, as if he were strangled every other day and wasn't worried about bodily harm. "It was all quite innocent enough."

"He wasn't there while I was dressing, Dailey," she said, hoping to prevent bloodshed. "He arrived after I'd put the boots on."

"Meh—" Hermes's taunt turned into a gurgle.

Payton leapt on Dailey's back and beat on his forearm attached to the hand gripping Hermes's neck. "Will you knock this shit off?"

Her mind grew fuzzy, and her toes became uncomfortably warm as a pink glow illuminated the hallway. Although fearful of what she'd see, she glanced down at her feet. Sure enough, the crystals were all alight.

The room spun. Panicked, she released him and backed away. "What's happening? Why do I feel lightheaded?"

Black dots started in her peripheral vision before her whole world went tits up.

With supernatural speed, Dailey dropped Hermes, caught Payton, and swept her into his embrace. His heart lodged in his throat.

She was so pale! He couldn't remember a time when she'd been sick.

"What's wrong with her?" he demanded, giving the Trickster a glare. "If those fucking boots did something to her, I will rip you apart and send you to Hell in pieces."

Hermes appeared perplexed as he stared at her face. "Does she have low blood sugar? She skipped breakfast to get here before you blew your load."

"Before I..." He huffed out a breath. "I left her coffee and—"

"Doesn't matter. She was frantic." There was no accusation in the God's tone, merely a gentle reminder for Dailey to consider that perhaps his deadline had produced these results. "From not taking the proper time to consume a meal, she may simply be weak."

With a shake of his head, he said. "I doubt it. She's skipped meals before, and this has never happened." He glared at Hermes. "As soon as I get her checked out, I'll be back to discuss what exactly these fucking shoes can do. You'd better make yourself available."

From nowhere, Tripp loomed large. "Making demands of my cousin will assure he fucks off to parts unknown. You'll never find him again." With a droll glance at Hermes, he added, "He's a rebellious child at best."

"You're one to talk!" Hermes scoffed. "How many centuries did you run from your fated mate?"

Ignoring him, the demigod held out his arms. "Give Payton to me. I'll take her to Elara and Florence."

Dailey's grip tightened involuntarily.

"Fuck off," he growled. "Send a doctor here."

Both gods smirked.

Dailey charged into his office, slammed the door with his heel, and laid Payton on the walnut leather couch she'd picked out for him when they'd first begun dating. As angry as he'd gotten, he couldn't bring himself to get rid of the damn thing. It had been one of the first gifts she'd bought for him, and the day they'd spent searching for the perfect furniture piece still ranked as one of his favorites. It was second only to the night he proposed and she accepted.

He grabbed the throw blanket, wadded it up, and stuffed it under her head. Perched on the sofa's edge, he brushed her hair back from her long, graceful neck and felt for a pulse.

Calm but strong, with no indication she was in peril. Still, he didn't love that she'd collapsed as she had. Payton wasn't the fainting sort.

Most women weren't, with the exception of pregnancy.

His stomach tightened, and he grew clammy.

Christ alive! He hadn't thought to ask if she was seeing anyone. Maybe she had a new lover wherever she resided now, one she was serious about. Three years was a long stretch to go without companionship.

He would know.

He'd been lonely from the moment she crawled out that window. Yes, he'd begun dating before the Hawthorne sisters' spell ruined his chances at finding love again, and he was thoroughly pissed his life had been derailed a second time. Yet those dates, while fun, hadn't sparked the joy he'd once known, and he'd been left feeling empty. Now, he had to ask himself, how angry did he have the right to be?

"No one has ever made me laugh like you, Pay," he confessed in a whisper, unsure why he did. Perhaps speaking to her unconscious state was the only way he could reveal his true feelings these days.

"You, Payton Hawthorne, are like the wildfire I nick-named you for, burning bright, consuming everything in your path, and leaving destruction in your wake." Dailey stroked her cheek, marveling at its silky smoothness. "But Goddess, I miss you," he added achingly.

Her lids twitched, as if she'd heard him, and he experienced another "oh shit" moment. It belatedly occurred to him that he was beginning to *feel* again: worry for her, anxiety on his behalf, longing for what once was.

But when did the happiness come? Hell, he'd settle for

being content. Anything but this relentless fury. Was he never to have peace again without her in his life? Why couldn't the Gods send him someone to love who would love him wholeheartedly, regardless of his pain-in-the-ass mother?

On many occasions since Payton had hightailed it out of town, Dailey ruminated on things he might've done differently. Rowan had been correct. His arrogance had been the wrecking ball to his perfect world. He'd just been too stupid to see it.

Self-reflection was a bitch. In the wee hours of the seemingly endless nights, he dwelled on all the "what ifs." And when morning dawned, he was more tired and soul-weary than when he'd gone to bed.

Payton's eyes opened just as Elara burst through the door, with Witchmere's newest doctor, Hope Weatherspoon.

"What happened?" Elara demanded, shoving him as she tried to reach her sister.

He refused to budge, earning a disbelieving glare from her, a quizzical frown from Hope, and a soft smile from Payton.

"Dailey?" Hope prodded when he didn't answer.

"She fainted after trying to pull me off of Hermes," he stated gruffly.

"Hermes!" Elara's gaze zeroed in on Payton. "What in the—"

"His fucking boots are back," Payton said, as she shoved the hair out of her eyes and sat up. "He felt the need to taunt Lee—er, Dailey, and our police chief, who's in a permanent bad mood, was triggered."

"Do you mind if I examine you, Ms. Hawthorne?" Hope asked, setting her black bag on the desk.

"That's not necessary," Payton demurred with an apologetic grimace. "I'm fine. Really."

Hope watched her for a moment, then addressed him. "How long was she out, Lee?"

Before respond, color surged up Payton's neck and into her cheeks. Hurt—dare he say betrayal?—flashed in they eyes she cast his way. He answered her stare with a raised brow. What had she expected? That he would remain a monk? For the first time in all their acquaintance, her eyes dulled, darkening from her bright aquamarine to deep-sea green.

A witch's tell.

Why did it bother him so badly? Shouldn't he be feeling nothing?

"Miss Haw—" Hope began.

"Please call me Payton." She offered a fake smile bearing no resemblance to her usual engaging grin. "But if you don't mind, I have to go."

"You're not going anywhere," Dailey snapped. His irritation with her stubbornness was rising, but he didn't credit it to her so much as his curse. However, he'd be damned if she was setting one foot out of this room without getting checked out first. "Let Hope examine you so we can discuss your charges from last night."

"Charges?" Elara's indignation electrified the air. "Are you talking about the trumped-up popcockery from last night, Dailey Knob?"

"Cobb," he ground out.

"Really? Because Pay said you were acting like a total—"

Payton clapped a hand over her sister's mouth, squeezing her eyes shut. "For the love of the Goddess, El, shut up."

Elara knocked her hand away. "No. He's not going to use his badge for nefarious means, all because you ditched him."

"Oh!" Hope squeaked. Their previous dinner conversation must've finally clicked. "Ohhhh. *She's* the one."

"Okay, I'm taking control of this little runaway train," Payton said as brightly as she could, considering. "Doc, other than a raging headache, I'm fan-fucking-tastic." She turned to her sister. "El, I'll handle my own messes this time, thanks."

"What about bail?" Elara asked with a concerned frown. "Who's going to get you out of the pokey?"

And suddenly it was all too much. The need to escape was upon him, to get away from the accusing eyes of all three women. Dailey dragged on his beanie, shrugged into his coat, and sailed out the door. He didn't stop until he reached the festively decorated sidewalk sign outside *Wily Witches Brew-Ha-Ha.*

Yes, he could've conjured coffee and a bagel for Payton, but her underlying pain struck a matching chord in him. With him out of the room, maybe she'd let Hope do her job and figure out why she'd fainted. And perhaps Elara wouldn't hex him with another year-long spell.

CHAPTER SIX

"Well, this is awkward," Payton muttered after she'd convinced Elara to leave.

The doctor was classically pretty, with old-money looks. The kind Dailey's bitch mother would approve. Mary-Alice Cobb had probably danced in her sensible-heeled shoes when he brought Dr. Hope Weatherspoon home.

"Isn't it just?" Hope replied dryly. "Are you ready to discuss why you fainted, or should we stretch this awkwardness even longer?"

"Look, no offense, but I'm not interested in having Dailey's girlfriend examine me, okay?" Payton surged to her feet. "You can tell him you did, and I promise, when I get back home, I'll follow up with my regular GP."

"I can't treat you if you don't want me to," Hope said evenly, "but I will say, I'm not Lee's girlfriend."

Hearing his nickname on another woman's lips sliced her open from stomach to breastbone. The searing pain was almost as horrific as the day she'd made the decision to leave Witchmere and everything she loved behind.

"Only people he's extremely close to call him Lee. Not even his mother or brother calls him that."

"I didn't say we hadn't been intimate," Hope replied coolly. "But I'm not currently his girlfriend. I suppose I never was."

Her eyes showed her quiet disappointment, a private truth she didn't bother to hide.

Payton could relate.

"I'm sorry." And weirdly enough, she meant it. Dailey was a good man. Considerate, loving, kind—or at least he had been before she did a number on him. "If it's any consolation, his distance is probably due to a spell, not anything you did or didn't do."

An amused smile curled Dr. Hope's mouth, but steady gaze remained serious. "I never believed I was the cause, Payton."

"Oh, well, that's good, then." What was it like to be so confident in who you were as a person? It wasn't something she was familiar with, despite the rebellious kiss-my-ass front she liked to put up.

"You seem to be fine, but I'll leave my card in case your symptoms return. Hydrate, rest, and keep your stress to a minimum." Hope's smile widened. "And yes, I believe it's probably simple dehydration. We all get a bit rundown after an epic party. Tripp and Elara's was legendary."

"His mother's doing, not my sister's or Tripp's. They aren't the type to host a town-wide shindig."

"Hm, yes, well, meddlesome mothers can be problematic."

Payton's brows shot up. "You've had experience in that department? Or was it our beloved mayor?"

"Both." Hope surprised her when she snorted. "It's disturbing how much our parents are alike."

The rub was that Payton found herself liking the woman. "You have my sympathy."

"Yes, well, I should've taken a page from your book and run away from the drama years ago." Hope froze the instant she registered what she'd said, and her hand flew to cover her mouth.

If the good doctor's face held even a smidgeon of malice, Payton would've eviscerated her. But her embarrassment was genuine. She waved it off.

"Don't stress it. I'm not offended by the truth."

Hope closed the distance between them and clasped her hand.

"I like you, Payton Hawthorne. I think we'd be great friends without the specter of dating Dailey hanging between us. If you ever want to grab a drink sometime, let me know."

"I doubt I'll be around that long."

"Ah, well, that's a shame. My office is two doors down if you change your mind about either the exam or the drink." She sniffed lightly. "Mm. Maybe you can tell me what perfume you use. It's delicious."

"I don't use perfume."

The doctor frowned, then nodded before picking up her bag and exiting.

After she was alone, Payton collapsed back onto the couch. Yes, she could leave, but she'd promised Dailey she would take her lumps, and it was exactly what she intended to do. Follow-through had never been her strong suit, and she couldn't shake the fact that she'd been a disappointment to him.

The door opened, and there he was, cheeks lightly flushed by the cold. He had a wary look in his eyes.

"Don't panic. Everyone's gone but the jailbird," she quipped. "Your girlfriend might have a word or two for you later, though."

Her teasing fell flat. Perhaps he recognized it as a probing question disguised as sarcasm. Payton wanted to believe Hope, but she'd seen the silent exchanges between the two. And she couldn't rule out the good doctor's *I didn't say we hadn't been intimate* comment.

"Are you trying to convince me you haven't had a lover in three years, Hawthorne? I'll call you a damned liar," he retorted with a scowl.

"Then call me a damned liar," she said softly.

Oh, she'd gone on a handful of dates, even kissed a few toads, but none were the prince standing before her, so she'd given up. Worse, while she had expected him to move on, it hurt like hell knowing he had.

A thoughtful frown drew his brows together, and he set the coffee carrier on the desk. He drew her to her feet and looked deeply into her eyes. "To clarify, you've never dated anyone else?"

"I didn't say that. I said I didn't take a lover since our breakup."

"How many?"

"How many what?"

His gaze swept over her face and settled on her lips. "How many did you date?"

"Four."

"Hm." He rubbed his thumb across her lower lip. "And did you kiss them?"

"They kissed me. I didn't initiate anything."

He nodded, as if it confirmed some inner theory of his, then said, "Good."

Dailey lowered his head, capturing her mouth in another of his bone-melting kisses. Her feet warmed, and fire swept through her veins. All she wanted was to get horizontal with him, but Dr. Hope became an intrusive thought, cooling Payton's ardor.

With a hand on his chest, she stopped their runaway sex train.

"I'm not the other woman, Dailey."

"No one said you were." He moved to dive back in, but she sidestepped. "What's this, Pay?"

She shrugged and lifted one of four red holiday cups from the carrier.

"It was sweet of you to get enough for everyone," she said instead of answering.

But then, that was part of the problem. His consideration. Only it hadn't been when it mattered—like with his mother.

"Hope isn't my girlfriend," he said quietly. "We dated steadily, but before feelings could grow, Elara's spell hijacked my emotions."

Payton's relief was a funny thing. In large part because she didn't want him to find someone else. Her flawed logic said, if she couldn't get over their relationship, he shouldn't be able to. It was unfair—some might say childish—but he'd imprinted on her soul, and her heart had claimed him as hers after their first meeting.

"I'm sorry." She faced him so he could see her sincerity. "She seems nice."

"She is. And she's reliable."

Her breath seized at the deliberate dig.

"Wow," she finally said. "It's hard to fathom how much you still hate me."

"I've already told you, I don't feel much of anything since the curse." He stormed forward and tipped up her chin. "You told Elara to 'take away the love he feels' and that you didn't want me to hurt anymore. But that love was woven into every fiber of my soul, Payton. And now, it seems, I don't possess one anymore."

And the blows kept coming!

Dailey didn't gain any satisfaction from her gasp or the shimmer of tears in her eyes. Hell, he wished he did. But once again, he felt hollowed out, as if the brief surges he's been experiencing over the last twelve hours had fizzled.

All except for desire. He couldn't seem to get a handle on his need to fuck her senseless. Maybe it was the dress, or possibly her particular brand of pheromones, but the drive to claim her again was unrelenting.

"There's a bagel for you. Eat up," he said, stepping away and putting the desk between them. "We can't have you fainting again."

"I'm not hungry."

He cast her a quick glance, noting how pale she seemed. Hurrying back to her, he urged her into the chair.

"If you won't let Hope check you out, let's find another doctor. You don't look well, Pay."

"You already told me you can't feel, Dailey. Cut the concern, okay?" Her voice was as tight as her expression. "Let's discuss the charges you intend to leverage against me. The legit ones, not resisting arrest. Instinctively hiding my hands doesn't count."

The tingling tickled his diaphragm, and he fought a grin. Sitting on the edge of the desk, he picked up a to-go cup and sipped it to hide his reaction. When he'd regained control, he said, "So the B&E and drunk driving are legit?"

Her eyes narrowed in irritation. "I'm not admitting to anything. That's what lawyers are for. But if you're going to charge me, do it now, or I'm going home. I have a bridal shower to plan for my sister."

The mention of Elara's planned wedding left a sour taste in his mouth, and he set the coffee aside.

"What did I say this time?" she snapped.

Her cluelessness was maddening.

"Oh, I don't know. Maybe it's hearing you say 'bridal' as if it's a throwaway word. I suppose to you, it is."

She surged to her feet and stabbed a finger into his chest. "Stop it, Dailey. Just stop!" Her voice bordered on a sob. "You know damned well I love you. But you did nothing to stop your mother from making sure I didn't feel good enough every chance she could. Do you really believe anyone can live through an entire lifetime of criticism without it extracting a price?"

"It wasn't a lifetime—"

"No, but it would've been," she said. "She hates me. There's no changing her mind. But whenever I tried to bring it up, you distracted me with romantic gestures and sex."

He stared at her empassioned visage, happy to see color in her cheeks again.

Happy.

Odd choice, all things considered.

But she'd made a valid point. Dailey dealt with strife throughout his day as a law-enforcement officer. He hadn't wanted to come home to complaints, too. In ignoring the problem, he was to blame.

He opened his mouth to apologize when something she said clicked.

"You love me?"

"Are you stupid, or did Elara's accidental curse steal what was left of your brain? Of course, I love you. Something so pure doesn't just go away." She shoved past him and headed for the door, intent on escaping.

His panic paralyzed him for all of five seconds.

"Payton!" The cry was ripped from him, and there was no disguising his desperation. It made him sick to hear it again, the ragged despair at her leaving. His nerve endings buzzed, and his vision grew cloudy.

In the next second, she was there, guiding him to the couch.

"Breathe, Dailey—"

"Lee," he blurted, as the piercing pain returned to his heart. "It will always be Lee for you, Wildfire."

Her eyes softened to match her smile. Just as she opened her mouth to reply, the door opened, and the visitor was one neither cared to see right then.

His mother took in the scene with a look of distaste. "What the hell is going on here? Get away from my son!"

CHAPTER SEVEN

"Your timing is impeccable, as always," Payton replied with a calm she didn't feel. She'd swear on a stack of grimoires the woman probably scryed each of their locations and, finding them together, intended to do everything in her power to keep them apart.

Mayor Mary-Alice Cobb carried herself with the rigid posture of someone who believed good breeding was a moral requirement and bad manners were a criminal offense. She was the perfect politician with a side of country-club queen. Everything about her was curated, from her immaculate chignon to the pearls she wore like armor. An ironclad self-righteousness simmered beneath her polished exterior, and her permanent sneer suggested everyone around her smelled faintly of disappointment.

And Payton hated the bitch.

The instant she met Dailey's suddenly wary gaze, she had an epiphany. The clarity of hindsight struck, making her realize he always wore either a hunted or a badgered look whenever his mother showed up.

How had she missed it before? Had she developed a sixth sense for these things recently?

Payton waited a few heartbeats for him to take control of the situation, but he remained quiet, watchful. And in between the silent beats, disappointment rode her hard. Apparently nothing had changed on his end, and he was still unwilling to stand up for her.

With a weary sigh, she climbed to her feet. "You know where to find me when you're ready, Officer Cobb."

She'd meant when he was ready to pull his head out of his ass, but he interpreted it as having to do with the incident from last night, because he said, "Don't leave town."

His hard-edge tone could only mean one thing—he intended to follow through with the charges.

A little of her old rebellious nature surfaced, and she said, "I already told you I have to plan my sister's bridal shower. But after that, no promises." With a middle finger flip, she picked up her bag from the floor and headed for the door.

The way was blocked by her nemesis.

"You aren't welcome here after what you did," Mary-Alice informed her.

Big surprise there!

"I know," Payton said with as much dignity as she could muster. There had been no excuse for running out on Dailey on their wedding day. She should've called a halt to their relationship long before.

But the old witch wasn't done. "You—"

"Mother!"

Her eyes burned with loathing, and despite Dailey's sharp reprimand, the mad cow was determined to continue. "You can crawl back—"

"Enough!" Dailey's roar shook the blinds, shocking both Mary-Alice and her.

Although he'd been formidable during their time together, he'd never been able to control his environment with only his voice. When had he become so powerful? And why was it so seductive, even now?

He continued as if he didn't realize the force of his anger. "I mean it, Mother. One more fucking word, and I'll pack my shit and go."

Mary-Alice gasped. A look of betrayal settled on her autocratic face. "Dailey!"

"No. You're done with the insults and insinuations. Payton has done nothing to deserve it." His expression was as stone cold as his words, able to freeze fire, and it left little doubt of his seriousness. Gray eyes, no longer dull and lifeless, sparked with rage. And surprise of surprises, it wasn't directed at Payton.

The desire to thank him was strong, but with her throat thickening, she couldn't speak. Yet he understood. Of course he did because he always saw more than anyone else.

Holding out his hand, he said, "We have things to discuss."

Deep-seated instinct urged her to take the olive branch, to place her palm in his, but she hesitated.

"We don't have time for this Dailey," Mary-Alice cut in with purpose. "We have a family emergency."

His cool gaze landed on his mother. "If it's not imminent death, I don't give a shit."

Payton's heart melted, but was his action of putting her first too little too late? Was there any way to salvage their trainwreck of a relationship after so long a break? She'd like to think so, but it didn't start with his alienating other family members who did matter, like Harrison or his sister Sloane.

"It's okay, Dailey," Payton assured him. "I'll wait."

He dropped his arm. "I'll pop around after I deal with whatever this is."

She nodded and hurried out without a backward glance.

"What the hell are you doing, Payton Hawthorne? Are you insane?" she scolded herself. She should book an appointment with Harrison and have her brain examined! Or maybe she should pray for a meteor to take Witchmere out. It was the only way she'd stop returning to this hellhole for another self-torturous cycle.

A fiery flash appeared in the sky, growing in size and speed until Payton feared her cursed boots brought her random thought to life. In a blink, it was gone, and at her feet lay a glowing green egg-shaped rock. The urge to pick it up was overwhelming, but if it had just burned its way through their atmosphere, wouldn't it fry her fingers? And yet, it hadn't melted the shoveled-packed snow it landed in.

"Fuck it."

Bending, she held her hand an inch from its scale-like exterior, and sensing no heat, she dared touch a finger to the surface. Although warm, it wasn't scalding hot.

"This is so not smart," she told herself as she scooped it up and cradled it between her palms to examine. "This is how all alien horror films start!"

"It's true. That was pretty dumb on your part."

Payton yelped and fumbled the egg, barely managing to catch it before it hit the pavement.

"Jesus, Rowan! You need a damned bell on your neck."

"Bells are for cats. Not wolves." Inching closer, she peered at Payton's prize. "I've never seen anything like it. But do they look like dragon scales to you?"

"How the hell would I know? I've never seen a dragon."

"Hm."

"Hm? Hm, what?"

Rowan shrugged. "Nothing. Just hm."

"Is it just me, or was the thing on fire before it landed?"

"I saw it, too." Her green eyes sparkled as she added, "I also heard what went on inside the station."

"It's those massive ears of yours," Payton quipped.

Her friend's hands flew upward to touch the appendages in question before she scowled and dropped them.

"God, you're a bitch."

Laughing for what felt like the first time in years, Payton bumped shoulders with her. "You know you're perfect, ho. Hell, all the women in this town want to *be* you, and all the men want to be *with* you."

"All but one," Rowan said with a morose glance down the street at Harrison Cobb's office.

"Yeah, well, his loss."

"Remind me again, why are those brothers brainless?"

Payton grinned as she tucked the green-scaled egg in her purse. "With a mother like Mary-Alice *Knob*, how can they be normal?"

"Cobb," someone ground out.

"Crap on a cracker, the non-future monster-in-law's behind me, isn't it?" she whispered.

"Yep," Rowan whispered back. "So's *Officer* Knob."

Daring a glance over her shoulder, Payton witnessed a flash of straight white teeth before Dailey sobered. Had his curse really been lifted? She wanted to ask, but couldn't find the courage to bring it up in front of his horrid mother. The miserable witch didn't need one more thing to hold over Payton's head.

"Excuse us, ladies." He did nothing to disguise the humor in his voice. "Lead on, Mother."

They hadn't made it two feet before Rowan called out, "Isn't she always leading you boys by your noses, Dailey?"

Mary-Alice's heels clip-clopped on the sidewalk as she trotted away, but Dailey wasn't so quick to follow.

"Careful, Rowan. If she takes it into her head to hex you, I can't stop her."

"What could she possibly do that I'd give a crap about?"

He turned around, walking backward while keeping them in his sights. "Ever see one of those Sphynx cats?"

Rowan paled.

Dailey shrugged.

And Payton laughed. How could she help it? The visual was priceless.

Across the distance, her eyes locked with his, and she was happy to see them come to life. With a wink and a whistle, he faced forward and jogged to catch up to his outraged mother.

Payton sighed.

"Don't," Rowan warned.

"What?"

"You know very well what. If you want your newly

healed heart carved out again, fall back in love with the man."

"It never healed, Ro. And I never fell out of love with him," she confessed.

Silence settled between them as they watched Dailey's fine ass strut away.

Finally, Rowan turned to her. "Should we bust your dragon egg open and see what's inside?"

"No! Talk about dumb!" Payton placed a protective hand over her purse. "There's no telling what we'd unleash."

"Fair. Let's get margarita mix and drown our sorrows instead."

For the first time, she didn't want to hang out with Rowan and drown her sorrows. Her need to be alone took precedence. "Can't. I have a few things to do. Can I meet you later?"

CHAPTER EIGHT

"Your sister has returned to town."

Dailey hated how cold his mother sounded, as if Sloane was only related to him and wasn't her daughter. "More's the pity for her."

"This is serious, Dailey!"

"Oh, I'm serious." His mother's betrayed glare triggered his sigh. Would he ever stop feeling like a recalcitrant schoolboy being scolded by her? "Is she dying? No? Has she murdered someone? Again no? Then tell me how is this life or death."

"I never said it was."

His frustration boiled over. At a crucial moment with Payton, his mother had barged in and chased her away. With another bout of clarity, Dailey recognized the power play. Understood that by not addressing her behavior and taking a stand, he'd let the best thing in life slip through his fingers. Why had he been so damned oblivious?

Sizzling above him caught his attention, and the smallest of flaming pebbles, barely discernible to the eye, headed straight for them. Stepping into his mother's space, he wrapped a protective arm around her and ushered them away from the danger zone. The stones, no bigger than those in a fish aquarium, fizzled on impact, having been snuffed out by the snow banks on either side of the walkway.

"What in the… I'll lay odds this is that Titan Tramp's doing!" His mother's outrage was complete. "She's always had it in for me, and now that she's facing prison time, she's trying to harm you, too, Dailey."

For the briefest of moments, he considered she might be right. But then shook off the drugged sensation swirling throughout his brain. As angry as Payton had been in the past, she'd never struck out at Mother or him. Even in the alley, on the day the Hawthorne sisters cursed him, her expression had been one of angst. And her words… he suddenly recalled the scene with an ache in his chest.

"You were engaged, and she loves you," Elara said, oblivious to the brewing storm.

"Elara! Please leave it alone," Payton urged frantically.

"No. He can't treat you like that. None of them can!" Elara stalked to her sister's side and gripped her hand. "Aren't you sick of it? I know I am. What do you want, sissy?" she asked.

"To take away the love he feels," Payton said in a raw voice. "I don't want him to hurt anymore."

She had never meant to curse him! She'd never understood the power her sister held. Then his mother's comment sank in. How the hell had she known he'd planned to level charges? Had she been eavesdropping?

Goddess, he was an idiot!

The tingling began, turning into a raging fire in his veins, and he cried out.

"What is it? Dailey?" His mother's concern penetrated his pain, and he had enough presence of mind to squeeze her hand, reassuring her he was all right. The burning wave washed over him, then faded, leaving him in a clammy-skin state.

"I have to go," he blurted.

"Go? No. We have to—"

But he didn't stay to listen. He had to find Payton to tell her he forgave her, both for running away and for the incident in the alleyway. He also needed her to forgive him for not being the man he should've been.

Dailey only managed half a block before he grew dizzy. The smell of his mother's perfume filled the air, overwhelming him, until he nearly gagged. Spinning back, he noted the intense concentration on her face as her lips moved in some silent enchantment.

Rage exploded inside his chest. Had it not been for Tripp stepping onto the path between Dailey and his mother, he wasn't sure what he'd have done.

Tripp threw up a hand to deflect the spell.

"His mother's mischief, meet my wall.
Return her straight to City Hall."

Mary-Alice blinked once, dropped her arms, and, looking for all the world like an animatron, stomped her way back to her office.

"What the actual fuck?" Dailey was appalled and in a

state of semi-disbelief. "She cast with me as her target! Why would she do that?"

Tripp's obsidian eyes held nothing but regret when they met his. "I suspect she sensed she's losing her hold over you, Cobb. Perhaps you and your siblings should meet to find sure-fire ways to protect yourselves moving forward."

"She's my mother," he said, shaking his head. "Mothers, they don't use magic against their children."

But his just had, and there was no telling how many times she'd done so.

"I'm sorry. Not all parents are the June Cleaver sort."

The ridiculousness of the demigod's response surprised a laugh from him.

"You watched *Leave It To Beaver*?" Dailey asked with a bark of laughter.

A wry smile followed Tripp's initial flush of embarrassment. "Yes, but only when I was feeling homesick and refused to head back to Messia to visit my parents. I'm entrusting this knowledge to you on penalty of death should you reveal it."

"Sorry, but the cat's out of the bag, Nightshade." Daily gestured with his chin, indicating the sudden appearance of the Trickster behind him.

"I thought I felt a migraine forming." Tripp shifted to allow Hermes into their circle. "What the hell do you want? Don't you have unsuspecting females to con in your cat form?"

"Do I want to know?" Dailey asked in an aside.

"Elara needed a friend. Loner that she was, it was natural she'd adopt a stray cat," Hermes replied with a smirk. "You're just jealous I was curled up to her for two years, and you weren't."

Thunder rumbled above them, and hail pelted Hermes with icy precision.

"Asshole," he muttered.

"You broke her heart, you dick," Tripp snapped. "She loved Hex."

Dailey did a double-take. "Wait, what? You pretended to be Hex? What happened to the real cat?"

"There never was one." Hermes shrugged carelessly. "It was just to protect her from predators."

Tripp took a threatening step toward him. "*You* were the predator, you bloody fool!"

Ignoring him, Hermes spoke directly to Dailey. "Why is your sky broken?"

"What?" He glanced between the cousins. "I thought Tripp instigated the hail."

"I'm not referring to his temper tantrum. I meant the mini meteor shower."

"The... Oh! The pebbles? Yeah, I don't know. It's one more thing I'll have to investigate today." As if he didn't have enough on his plate! But if someone were a threat to the residents, they needed to be stopped. This close to the holiday, there were additional tourists, too, and they couldn't risk exposing their secrets.

Amusement flared in the Trickster's impossibly green eyes, making them look like polished emeralds. They also made Dailey uneasy.

He scowled. "What am I missing?"

"When I can prove my theory, you'll be the first to know." With a wink and a jaunty grin, Hermes strolled away.

"I'm beginning to hate that guy," he muttered.

"You should. He had designs on Payton."

Dailey bristled as he whipped around to stare at Tripp. "What the fuck are you talking about? When? While she and I were together?"

FWOOOOOOOOSH—

A blazing rock ripped through the fabric of space overhead, heading straight for the *"Welcome to Witchmere!"* sign. It burst into flames, eliciting shouts from passersby.

"Sonofabitch!"

"I'll take care of it," Tripp offered. "You find your siblings and get an anti-Mother ward in place. You're going to need it when my enchantment wears off."

"Right. Thanks."

After checking both ways for vehicles, Dailey jogged across the street toward his brother's office.

"Isn't that jaywalking?" Rowan called out. "Or doesn't the law apply to you?"

"Don't you have a job, Wolfy? Or is it to stand around and attract unsuspecting tourists with your honey trap?" he taunted. "Once they realize you're all vinegar and no sweet, they'll hightail it."

"You'd know all about hightailing hotties, Officer Knob," she retorted, making him laugh.

Call him a masochist, but he found her brand of sass delightful. Put her and Payton together, and it was a riot. Or it had been. Wildfire and Wolfy, he'd nicknamed them. Both befitting their personalities. Nostalgia for the good ol' days struck him, and he acknowledged his emotions were returning in full force. He sobered as he recalled those nights they'd all hung out. Back before rings and ultimatums ruined everything. And somewhere along the way, Rowan's snarky humor had veered toward mean and all directed at him or his family. With good reason, it seemed.

"You laughed," she said, approaching him with a deep frown. "That's twice today you broke your sourpuss mood. What gives?"

"I'm not sure, but I think the Hawthorne sisters' curse might finally be wearing off."

"Curse? What are you talking about? Neither Payton nor Elara would do such a thing. They're too soft. Me? Sure. Them, nah."

"Good to know who I need to keep an eye out for," he said dryly.

Her expression became earnest. "Please, Dailey. Don't break her heart again."

"She broke mine, Rowan."

"You should've stood up to Mary-Alice. Only you can."

"I'm not so sure," he replied with a thoughtful look at City Hall. His mother was backlit in her office window overlooking the street below.

"What's that supposed to mean?" Rowan demanded with hands on hips. "You're either man enough to stand up for your woman, or you're a wuss. Which is it?"

He met her angry gaze. "I always believed I was the first. But I think the Hawthornes aren't the only ones who enacted a spell."

Nonplussed, Rowan dropped her arms and followed his line of sight to the mayor's office.

"Dailey! What are you saying? Your mother interfered?"

"You tell me. What do you smell?"

"Other than burnt bread coming from *The Enchanted Oven*?"

He snorted. "Poor Willa. She can't seem to master her gran's recipes, can she?"

"She should sell the place to an actual baker." Rowan's grin flashed. "But she won't because everyone in Witchmere has her convinced she should be on that British bake-off show."

"It's by the grace of the Goddess she doesn't poison someone. I really should shut her down." Dailey shuddered.

"You missed your chance. You should've done that while you didn't have a heart," Harrison said as he joined them. His eyes practically threw hearts as they locked on Rowan, but only those who knew him well would see it. "Sanderson."

"Knob." With a flip of her long, red locks, she pivoted on her heel and stalked away.

"You didn't answer me," Dailey called.

With an irritated look and a grimace, she returned. "Step back, Harrison," she ordered. "I can't get any other scent with you poisoning the air."

His brother's mouth kicked up on one side before he quickly suppressed it and retreated a few yards away.

Eyeing them both with suspicion, Rowan leaned in, sniffed, and recoiled.

"Yeah, holy shitballs, dude. It's like you bathed in your mother's perfume or something. And if that's your thing, I ain't judging. Much." With a casual wave, she trotted away.

"What was that all about?" Harrison asked, his gaze locked on Rowan's retreating form.

"Don't tell me you didn't overhear us. Otherwise, you

wouldn't have made the comment about my heart, as accurate as it was." Dailey stepped between his brother and the object of his obsession. And why did it bother him more to suspect his brother of wrongdoings than their mother? "We need to talk. Can you text Sloane and get her to teleport to your inner sanctum? I'm assuming it's warded against outside influence and soundproof?"

"Yeah." His brother's expression screamed concern. "Should we include Mother? Is this an attack on—"

"No!" They both winced at his shouted response. A few passersby shot them curious looks. "Uh, no. I, uh… Ah, shit, Harry. If what I'm beginning to suspect is true, we have a real problem."

"Okay, let's get off the street." Pulling out his phone, Harrison shot off a text. A few seconds later, a chime indicated Sloane's response. "She'll be here in five."

CHAPTER NINE

"What's going on, Dailey?" Sloane asked the second she stepped over the threshold to Harrison's office.

"This is going to sound insane," Dailey began.

"Well, you're in the proper place for it," she quipped.

"Funny, now may I finish?"

Although she smirked, she remained silent.

Drumming up his courage, he said, "I think Mother is manipulating us with magic."

Harrison's met in the center of his forehead, and Sloane's perfectly penciled brows rose.

"You were always her staunchest supporter, D. What's changed? Why are you bringing this to us now?" she asked, tucking a silky strand of her chestnut hair behind her ear and ruining the bob's precision cut with the casual action. By displaying her earlobe, she also revealed a one-carat diamond of the finest quality. Another flawlessly put-together Cobb among their line. No one could look at any of their family and see them for the actual mess they were.

"Tripp interrupted her mid-enchantment."

"And Rowan recoiled when she smelled Mother's perfume on him," Harrison added. "A light touch wouldn't have created so visceral a reaction."

"Wait, you and Rowan are a thing?" she asked Dailey.

"No! God. I wouldn't do that to Harry."

A flush of color painted their brother's cheekbones, reinforcing his embarrassment at being called out about his life-long crush. "She doesn't see me that way," he said, with all the dignity he could muster.

Dailey hurt for him. Unrequited love sucked. "Maybe. Maybe not. But I'm not going there, ever. I value my balls too much, and she'd bust them every chance she got."

"Look, I've no love for our mother. As you both know, she's made my life a misery. But the evidence sounds circumstantial to me." So saying, Sloane crossed to the window and peered toward City Hall. "I'm not saying she's not capable, mind you, but we need actual proof before we accuse her."

She hadn't been able to hide the suspicion or disdain in her voice, and her thoughtful gaze was laser-focused. Both signs his sister was nursing her own brand of resentment toward their mother.

"It was Tripp who suggested we ward ourselves against her as a precaution." Dailey dropped another WTF-bomb by saying, "And I agree."

But neither reacted as expected. Sloane nodded, while Harrison went to a bookcase behind his desk and drew down a novel. Surprise of surprises, the entire damn wall shifted, revealing a hidden ceremony room.

"Dude." Sloane laughed. "For the one who prefers to live like a mortal among witches and warlocks, you've shocked the hell out of us. I mean, who knew you had a secret spell room?"

Sage curled through the air in soft spirals from a small ceramic burner in the corner. The air was made thicker with the herb-sharp scent of rosemary. Completing the trifecta was the smoky sweetness of cedar wafting through the tiny room and flowing into the surrounding walls. Mary-Alice Cobb, with her primordial magic, might bully her way through the wards, but she wouldn't enjoy the price tag.

Dailey sniffed. "And what protection ward are you using? It smells fierce."

"One from Florence Shaw."

Both he and Sloane spun back to gape at Harrison. Flo and Mary-Alice had a longstanding feud. If their mother suspected he'd gone to her enemy for help, Harrison might as well change his last name and leave Witchmere.

"Be careful, Harry," Dailey warned. "I mean it."

"Mother has never paid attention to me before. I doubt she'll get a bee in her bonnet to start now." He shrugged as if the power of their ancestral line couldn't wipe their tiny town off the map. Hell, it had created it!

"Okay, so you boys are better versed with all this hocus pocus than I am. How do we protect ourselves? I've used distance in the past, but now I'm back here at the source, I'd like something foolproof," Sloane said as she thumbed through Harrison's grimoire. "Is this a replica of the Cobb original?"

"Yes," Harrison replied, leaning against the jam and crossing his arms as he watched them inspect the space.

Dailey joined Sloane, impressed despite himself. His little brother was far more clever than he'd ever realized, and twice as stealthy.

"What about charming amulets?" he suggested. He shot a quick glance at Harrison. "Blood from the three of us, infused in stones, all working together. The strength of the three outweighs the one."

Harrison nodded slowly as if mentally examining all the angles. "It could work, but it could also backfire if she discovers what we did and somehow breaks the bond."

Sloane looked up sharply. "You mean hurting one can hurt the other two?"

"Precisely."

She worried her lip, then gave a decisive nod. "I'm willing to risk it. I'm tired of her machinations and want to be free of her."

"Same," Dailey agreed. "Harry?"

"I'm in."

He hadn't realized how much he wanted—hell, *needed*—their support until right that second. But he was so fucking grateful for it.

"You do understand she'll try to dig her claws in and hold on to you the tightest, D, right?" Harrison asked. "You need to be prepared."

Dailey scrubbed his hands over his face. "Jesus! I've been asking myself all day how I never saw it. I feel like a turnip-brained toad."

"You love her, D," Sloane said. Wrapping her arms around his waist, she rested her glossy head on his shoulder.

"It's harder to see when you're so close." She drew back and cupped his jaw. "But it's a betrayal of us anyway you look at it."

"It's difficult to deny the bond between a firstborn and their mother. But what made you aware of her nature today, of all days?" Harrison watched him with undisguised curiosity. The doctor in him was already examining his motives and reasoning.

"Don't analyze me unless asked," he ground out. Dailey wasn't prepared for anyone to peel back the layers of his emotional onion quite yet. He had to live in his newfound feelings for a bit.

"I wouldn't dream of it. I'm curious about the catalyst, whether external or internal," Harrison replied mildly.

"Could be external. I'm thinking it has something to do with the Trickster's boots."

"Trickster Boots?" Sloane asked.

Harrison's calm dipped. "Shit. Not again."

"Yep."

"Who?"

"Payton."

Payton was halfway back to Elara's old apartment when she decided she didn't really want to be alone to lick her wounds. If things went as expected, with her life heading straight down the crapper, a few margaritas with Rowan would be a pleasant memory to dust off now and then.

After shooting off a text, she headed for *The Winking Wyvern* pub. She was ten feet away from the entrance when a shadow passed over the sun. The window-rattling roar from directly above was disconcerting, as was the rapidly warming air melting the snow into a puddle at her feet.

The sound of heavy flapping, like canvas in a gale, caught her attention, and she glanced around for the source. That's when she saw him, and holy dragon fire, was he a sight!

Screams rent the air, drawing the midday bar crowd out to investigate. The creature dove straight for her like a falling star, but her self-preservation took a holiday so she could take in the sheer magnificence of the beast. For a split second, Payton considered the possibility of a magical-boot hallucination, but others were running away or frozen, gaping at it, too.

Then, *he* landed.

The dragon shifted mid-step onto the sidewalk, landing in human form, naked, with smoke curling off his tanned, tattooed skin. The symbols, like nothing she'd ever seen, went from glowing to ink in a blink.

"Where are my children?" he growled, sending shivers throughout her body and causing onlookers to squeak in fear.

But his magic called to her Titan blood, and fool that she was, she threw caution to the winds as something remarkably like courage stiffened her backbone.

"Look, buddy, I don't know what that ridiculous entrance was all about, or where these so-called children of yours are, but you can't go around terrorizing others with your raging display of..." She made the mistake of glancing down his body. "Holy dragon dicks, dude!"

When she could tear her eyes away and meet his, there was a distinct twinkle in those amber depths.

"You were saying?" His voice was like velvet dipped in danger.

"I was?" she asked, distracted by the way the sunlight shone off his sculpted chest. And when he ran his hand through his dark, jaw-length hair like Fabio on an 80s romance cover, her ovaries sighed.

The man was broader than a barn, half feral, and barefoot.

In other words, perfect.

It had to be the whole Dragon Daddy vibe, gray streak and all, right?

"It would help if you were clothed, Vorren," a deep, amused voice said from behind her.

"Hermes." With a wink for Payton, Vorren the Viking-like Dragon Daddy—this is likely how she would always view him in her mind—snapped his fingers, clothing himself in a casual black, muscle-enhancing tee-shirt that high-lighted all the perfectly placed ridges a woman loved to ogle, and a pair of jeans. His feet were left bare.

"Won't your toes freeze? Dragons don't have to worry about frostbite?" And why did she care?

"Roll up your tongue, Payton," Hermes ordered with a light laugh. "We have work to do, my dear."

"Work?" She glanced up at him. "What work? I'm going in for a margarita with—"

"Holy fuckballs!"

Rowan had arrived, and her eyes were locked on Vorren the Vision.

"I know. They don't make them like that here in Witch-mere," Payton agreed.

Hermes frowned. "I'm a god."

"Yeah, but you don't count," she said, giving him a pesky-fly wave. "No one trusts you enough to boink you."

"That one really hurt." And damned if he didn't appear wounded.

"You're the one gifting town-destroying boots. What woman wants a pair of gorgeous shoes with a warning label?"

Vorren grinned. "At it again, Hermes?"

"Stuff it."

"Oh, I've got something he can stuff," Rowan said in a low, only meant for my bestie to hear voice.

Too bad both Hermes and Vorren, the Viking-like Dragon Daddy, had supernatural hearing.

Their amused laughter sent Rowan flying into the bar.

"It's her fight or flight instinct," Payton explained lamely. "Okay, nice chat. Try not to scare the residents, Dragon Daddy. Later."

He stepped into her path and placed a hand on her shoulder. "You have something of mine."

Dailey appeared from the alley beside the bar.

"You're going to want to remove that hand before I break every bone you possess," he growled.

A second later, a baseball-sized meteor shot straight for Dragon Daddy's head.

CHAPTER TEN

Vorren did the unexpected—and swoonworthy—by catching the flaming ball inches from his face, then crushing the rock to dust.

Payton gasped, positive she was dreaming.

Behind him, a wide-eyed Rowan had her nose pressed to the glass door, miming "Did you just see that shit?"

Ignoring her, Payton stepped closer to examine Dragon Daddy's hand.

No burn!

"How are you alive right now?" she asked, a little freaked the man appeared invincible. She glanced up. "And why are we being pelted with rocks?"

"Your mate is unstable," Vorren said with a pointed look at Dailey.

"Mate? He's not my—" She gulped as Dailey's expression darkened. "Oh. Wow."

Hermes eased Payton away from Vorren before facing

Dailey. "Law Dog, you need to control your temper. You're causing sky tantrums."

"What the hell are you talking about? They aren't coming from me."

FWOOOOOOOOSH—FWOOOOOOOOSH.

Vorren dove, snatching two flaming balls out of midair like he was an MVP catcher for the Yankees.

Dailey paled. "I am! Why is this happening?"

"My guess?" Hermes pointed to the boots. "Titan magic mingled with Trickster and warlock."

"For fuck's sake!"

FWOOOOOOOOSH—

Thankfully, Vorren was alert and saved the bar from certain disaster.

"Take a damned Valium, Lee, or you're going to destroy Witchmere." Payton impulsively reached for him and, in the process, slammed her tote into his stomach.

"Oomph!" He coughed and wrapped an arm around his middle. "Jesus, Pay. What the hell is in that bag? A brick?"

"Oh!" She drew out the egg and examined it for cracks. Finding none, she breathed a sigh of relief. "I was so worried you broke it."

"Me?" he choked out.

"The egg is mine," Vorren said.

She held it tighter. "Prove it."

His dark brows shot up a second before he frowned. "How do you expect I should do that? Other than shifting into my dragon form again?"

"No, I already know what you are. I have eyes, Dragon Daddy. But you'll need to prove it's your egg. This could be a rival dragon's egg, and you're trying to decimate their entire line."

He closed his eyes and rubbed the spot between his brows.

"It's his," Hermes confirmed. "The magical signature is exactly the same." But he frowned as he glanced at the bar entrance. "Is your mate in the pub, Vorren? There's an additional echo coming from someone inside."

"My mate is dead," he replied flatly. "She left me to protect our three unborn."

"Three?" Payton gave her prize a sorrowful glance, then turned it over to Dragon Daddy. "I was really hoping to see it hatch."

"There is something seriously wrong with you," Dailey said. But he clasped her hand and squeezed to show he was only teasing. Leaning in, he lowered his voice and said, "I'm curious what it would look like, too."

"Curiosity kills. Or it will in this case," Hermes said. "You don't want to be in the vicinity when a dragon egg hatches. The supercharged sulfurous purge will suffocate you and burn your eyes from their sockets."

"To put Payton's mind at ease, let's go speak to the other signature's owner, shall we?" Dailey suggested. The underlying steel in his tone said it wasn't a suggestion.

"Good. I need a pitcher of margaritas," she said with feeling.

He opened the door and gestured Vorren in, holding Payton back as Hermes followed.

"Wait a second, Wildfire," Dailey said.

"What's up? Is there a Payton booze ban, because I'm not down with that today."

His grin flashed.

In a lightning-strike moment, it registered what was different about him.

"The curse has lifted!"

"I believe so, yes. I also believe it should've worn off a long time ago, but someone prevented it." His expression read as forbidding, and Payton's stomach flipped.

Surely he didn't believe it was her fault, did he?

"No," he said, reading her reaction correctly. "I don't think you're to blame. If I had to guess, I'd say my mother is."

"Holy craptastrophe, that's a helluva jump, Lee. Why would she?"

"To keep me angry with you."

She closed her eyes against the truth, tired to her soul. Of *course* Mary-Alice would do whatever it took to keep them apart. Hadn't she been at it since day one?

"That's awful," Payton said softly. "I'm so sorry. If I had any clue we'd accidentally cast a lasting enchantment that day, I'd have made sure Elara removed it. I swear."

"I know, Pay. I think I always have."

"How did you find out about your mom?"

"Mother. The word mom indicates someone with feelings who actually values their children," he said tightly.

The pain in his eyes spoke of disillusionment, and she wished she could erase it. Standing on tiptoe, she touched her lips to his in a tender kiss.

"I'm sorry," she whispered.

Pressing his forehead to hers, he smiled. "You really have to stop apologizing for things out of your control."

"This is a major about-face from last night when you were ready to lock me up and throw away the key."

"If I lock you up, I want to be in the room with you. *Then* I'll toss the key."

She laughed, because this was the old Dailey, the guy with the naughty quips and wicked grins. The man she loved to distraction.

"We should see about our new dragon infestation," she suggested.

He pointed at the bar's signage. "I suspect our guy has been hiding under our noses the whole time."

She glanced up.

The Winking Wyvern.

"Cory?"

"Yeah. What does anyone know of his past? He breezed in here four years ago and bought this place, without ever revealing a thing about himself."

"And everyone accepted him because of his charming personality."

"Got it in one."

"Lead on, Officer Knob," she said.

"You and Rowan should really come up with a new nickname for me."

Turning toward the door, she shot him a flirty smile over her shoulder. "Oh, I don't know. I've always liked your knob."

Dailey enjoyed the view as Payton sauntered into the bar.

It had only taken the lessening of Elara's spell for him to remember how much he adored her. Although they both seemed to enjoy this new flirtation, a helluva lot needed to be resolved before they could mend their relationship, if they ever could.

It still boiled down to one thing: she left him at the altar. At any point, they could've mutually ended things to save him the embarrassment of facing a roomful of their loved ones and having to explain she'd climbed out a window rather than marry him. How was he supposed to reconcile the past to move into the future?

His heart contracted, and he fought to breathe. Why did it hurt just as badly, reliving the moment?

"Lee?"

Payton returned and laid her palm on his chest, easing the restriction. "What's wrong? Are you okay?"

"Why wouldn't he be with a babe like you?" a passing construction worker asked, adding a wolf whistle.

"Yeah, baby, why don't you ditch the loser and welcome a real man?" his friend called out.

A third opened his mouth, but the catcall turned into a screech as he spotted an entire arsenal of flaming rocks heading his way.

"Conniventia et duratus!" Payton shouted, instinctively encasing the mini meteor shower in water and freezing them. They still landed, likely stinging where they struck the men, but at least the trio didn't turn into Roman candles.

"Nicely done," Dailey rasped, finding it difficult to wrap his head around his latest ability to rain down hell.

"Why now?" she asked, her eyes studying him with concern. "And where did all the perverts come from?"

"In answer to both questions, I don't know," he admitted.

"Is Mary-Alice's best-behavior charm breaking down?"

He barked a laugh. "She never enacted one of those. Where did you get that idea?"

"This place was always too idyllic, as if everyone were under an enchantment to make this the perfect wonderland."

Was it? Dailey couldn't seem to recall.

"It doesn't matter. Let's find the egg's magical echo, get a drink, and maybe see if anyone has a spare chill pill for you."

"It's illegal to—"

"Dude, really? You've got emotion-activated astral discharges popping off without any warning, and you're worried about the legality of one prescription pill?" Without a by-your-leave, she ripped the badge from his chest and stuffed it in her purse. "You'll get it back when you aren't trying to murder everyone who triggers you."

"When did you get so bossy?" he asked, barely suppressing a chuckle.

"Not sure, but I think it was over the last twelve months. I'm a take-charge kind of gal now."

"I like it." And he did. Although rebellious in the past, she tended to follow where Rowan or Dailey led. Rarely had she actually stood up for herself, preferring to flip someone off and flee. Not dissimilar to her best friend. Both women had a strong flight gene.

Payton rolled her eyes. "Yeah, right."

"No, I do. Don't take this the wrong way, but you've grown up." He tipped up her chin. "And at our age, it's about time, wouldn't you say?"

Hurt was reflected in her eyes, and her compressed mouth said she had no intention of telling him he'd bumbled it.

"Talk to me, Wildfire. Please don't bottle it up. Not again."

"If I open that can, worms will explode in every direction," she confessed.

He understood, but he also knew if she didn't voice her feelings aloud, they'd never resolve a damned thing. Drawing her into his embrace, he kissed her temple. "We'll start small. Maybe let one out at a time, deal with it, then bring out another. Does that work for you?"

She paused to consider, nodding when she finally reached her decision.

CHAPTER ELEVEN

When they entered *The Winking Wyvern,* the owner was coming from the store room with a box of beer in his arms. His sharp gaze scanned the room, doing a double-take after landing on Vorren. A mixed bag of emotions crossed his face: shock, delight, pain, resignation. Finally, he settled on cautious, as he set the carton on the beer cooler with a light rattle of bottles.

Payton eased closer to overhear as the two approached each other.

"Well, look who crawled out of the volcano," Cory drawled. "You've aged terribly."

"Yes, well, you smell like cheap alcohol and poor decisions, Corvack."

"The ladies seem to love it."

They broke into grins, and Cory held out a hand, pulling Vorren in for a quick hug. Once they'd effectively pounded the crap out of each other's backs, the way only men can, they released each other.

"What are you doing in Witchmere? Last I heard, you were at the palace, deciding whether to abdicate your throne in favor of drowning in grief."

Payton cast Dailey and Rowan a wide-eyed glance.

"Throne?" Rowan mouthed.

Other than a shrug, Payton had nothing to give.

"We both know a dragon without his mate is useless, Corvack."

"My sister would hate to see you this way," Cory said with a flash of sorrow. "She'd want you to live your life to the fullest, old friend."

"Yes, well, my brother, Thorryn, will make a better king when the time comes. He has the temperament, and I no longer have a wife to rule by my side."

The brothers-in-law eyed each other for a long moment as if sharing a silent communication.

"Come, have a drink. They have something in this realm known as Fireball. You'll love it," Cory assured him.

He lined up shots on the bar, accounting for their whole group. "Cobb? You in or are you on duty?"

"I'm in."

Payton whirled to gape at him.

But Rowan wasn't letting him off easily. "Really, Officer Knob? What *will* your mother say?"

"I don't give a fuck what she says," he growled, and without breaking eye contact with Payton, said, "Make mine a double, but I'll have a whiskey, neat."

A thrill raced through her. What the hell did it mean?

Was he feeling reckless because he was sick of Mary-Alice's shit, or were the boots influencing him in some small way?

"No shot for me," Payton finally managed. "I'll have a margarita, on the rocks, salted rim."

"I'll have what she's having, but I'm not passing up a free shot," Rowan declared, sidling up to Vorren. "So, tall, dark, and dangerous, how do you drown your sorrows these days? I'm single in case you care to mingle."

"Oh, Jesus," Dailey said for Payton's ears alone. "Remind me why she's your friend again?"

"I can hear you, Officer Knob," Rowan snapped. "And she's my friend because I'm lovable and charming. Something you wouldn't know anything about."

Payton put a hand on his arm. "I've got this." In a blindingly fast move, she tapped Rowan on the back of the head. "Knock it off. He's been under a spell."

"Still is," Vorren stated matter-of-factly, toasting Cory with his second shot. "You were correct. This drink should be served with every meal. You would make millions of pyra at Drakoryth's annual Emberborn Gathering."

"It's Fireball, and I deal in dollars here." Cory poured two more shots and left the bottle. "Two margaritas and whiskey coming right up."

Payton leaned against the bar, inching sideways to make room for Dailey to join her.

"Where did Hermes go?" she asked as she craned her neck to see the room's occupants.

"Hermes? The black-haired devil always stirring up trouble in here? Never saw him," Cory replied, as he built her drink. "But then, he's been banned for over a month."

"What did he do?" Rowan asked.

"Wait, didn't he enter before us?" Dailey asked.

Cory halted mid-salting of the glasses to scan the place. Anger caused his topaz eyes to burn, and a tattoo on his neck glowed to match his irises.

"Holy shit, I think he spotted him." Rowan spun on her stool, following his gaze. "You'd never know that blond was him until he looked up. Those peepers are a dead giveaway."

In one fluid move, Cory cleared the bar, charging toward his nemesis.

Hermes, sensing his future existence was questionable, shimmered away, leaving a seat of stardust in his place.

"He fucking knows I hate that glittery shit!" Cory growled.

Vorren's laugh rumbled out, causing the glasses overhead to clink whenever they touched. "Some Gods never change, yes?"

"He's a menace," Dailey agreed.

"So he hung around here after the incident last Christmas with my sister?" Payton asked, accepting her cocktail from the backup bartender. "Thanks," she said with a moan after sipping it. "This is the best I've ever had."

He leaned in, elbows on the bar, blue eyes clearly interested. "Oh, you haven't had the best yet, lady. Not until you've had me."

Dailey froze.

Rowan snorted.

And Vorren, Goddess love him, shoved the bartender over with an open palm. "She has a mate, fool."

"I do?" Payton asked.

"She does?" Rowan perked up.

"Who?" Dailey ground out with a scowl.

"Yes, yes, and you, Law Dog," Vorren replied, popping the pour spout from the Fireball and drinking it straight.

"Christ, not you too with that Law-Dog shit." Snatching the bottle from his hand, Dailey swigged it.

"Is that not your name?"

"No! Hermes rotates nicknames in his never-ending attempt to get under my skin."

"Ah, it seems he has succeeded." Vorren nodded sagely, but there was a distinct sparkle in his gaze as he swiped the Fireball back. "You are very thin of skin, as they say."

"Thin-skinned, and no, I'm not."

"This is what I said. Thin of skin." So saying, Dragon Daddy downed the remaining two-thirds of the alcohol, sighed with satisfaction, and pinned Payton with a stare. "You are not attractive to me. I shall help you."

Dailey stood straighter, his body practically vibrating with outrage. "Not attractive?"

"Careful, Law Dog, you do not want more projectiles from your sky," Vorren warned. "My comment was not meant to be offensive to your mate. But I do not wish to fuck her. Or any of your people here. The women from my realm are more to my liking." He grinned as if it took the sting away.

"Why do I need you as a bodyguard?" Payton asked as she wove her fingers through Dailey's and squeezed.

"Look around you. Do you not smell the interest?"

"Smell the...?" Dropping Dailey's hand, she slowly spun to take in the room. Everyone was focused on her. Heat burned in their gazes as they swept over her body, and a few of the bolder men licked their lips. "Ohmygod, what the fuck?"

"They know you are ripe for breeding," Vorren replied with a shrug. Leaning over the bar, he grunted. "Corvack, your server is lazy. He is sleeping on the floor."

"Maybe because you cracked his head on the cabinet, you feral hatchling!" Cory snapped as he dumped a dustpan of glitter in the garbage.

Payton's mind was reeling. Ripe for breeding? What the hell was Dragon Daddy talking about? Sure, she hadn't had sex since Dailey, but that didn't mean she wanted to spawn little baby Titans anytime soon—if at all!

Worse, was Dailey only being nice to her because somehow the Trickster's chaos-causing boots had enchanted him? Her heart literally ached in her chest because suddenly, she was positive it was the case. Last night, before she'd slipped them on, he was all business. This morning, he'd drifted closer to his charming self. Not ten minutes ago, she believed they'd broken Elara's spell, but now, Payton was convinced whatever power she possessed amplified the boots' magic, likely overriding their previous faux pax from the alley incident.

"It's okay, Wildfire," he said, cradling her face with his warm palms. "I'll take you to my cabin and—"

"No!"

He dropped his arms, his expression becoming guarded. "You can't go out unprotected, Payton."

"Vorren can protect me. He said himself that he doesn't find me attractive."

"There is no way in hell you're going off with a strange

man twice your size with the strength of a mountain. I forb—"

"Watch it," she warned. "I'm not yours to command, Dailey Cobb."

"Be smart about this. He's a stranger you met all of fifteen minutes ago."

"I can go with her," Rowan offered, wrapping an arm around Payton's shoulders. "She—" Leaning closer, she sniffed. "Wow! What shampoo are you using these days? You smell divine."

Payton closed her eyes in resignation.

"No, really, Pay, I never realized how pretty you are. I mean, we both know men suck, so we should—eek!"

Vorren picked up Rowan in a fireman's hold. "Corvack, the little wolf needs to be contained. Do you have a storeroom?"

"If you don't put me down, I swear to the Goddess I'm going to rip your fucking throat out with my teeth," she growled. "I won't need to shift to do it."

He huffed out a laugh.

"What's so damn funny?"

"You are. To think, a creature as puny as you believing you can harm *me*."

Even Cory grinned, triggering Payton's curiosity.

"Is your skin tougher than rope?" she asked. "Because I've seen her gnaw through a three-inch strand."

"It's impenetrable," Cory explained. When she narrowed her eyes in disbelief, he lifted a knife and sliced it across his palm. Or attempted to. The blade broke off the handle and clanked to the floor. His flesh remained intact.

"Uh, guys." They all looked to where Dailey pointed.

The patrons were inching closer, hyper-focused on Payton, amorous intent in their eyes.

"Ohmygod!"

"Fuck it." Dailey wrapped an arm around her, and in a blink, they were in a living room she'd never seen.

CHAPTER TWELVE

Rage boiled inside Payton, and she whirled to face Dailey.

"What the hell gives you the right?" she demanded. "I already told you no."

"Look, you may not trust me to have your best interests at heart, and that's fine. But I'm still the police chief of this town, and my removing you from the scene was twofold."

He paused, giving her a chance to respond.

She merely lifted her brows, waiting.

With a deep sigh, he continued. "Okay, one, the situation was becoming threatening without an immediate solution. Two, you were in danger, and your safety, more than anything, prompted me to act. I won't have you hurt. Full stop."

"But you missed an important point."

Dailey frowned. "Which was?"

"You're as affected by whatever this mass hypnosis is as the people at the bar were."

"What the hell are you talking about?"

"Dailey, can you honestly tell me you don't want to rip my clothes off right now?"

"No, I can't." When she would've pressed for the win, he cut her off. "Of course, I want to, Wildfire," he said huskily. "I always have. Nothing has changed for me. Even when I was at my angriest, I was obsessed with you. I had plans to bring you back here, drive you mad with want, and make you beg me to make love to you."

"You're not making me feel any better." And he wasn't. Obsession, in any form, was cause for concern. Although she couldn't honestly say she wasn't just as crazy about him. But the truth needed to be laid bare. "In addition to wondering if you're lusting after me because of these fucking boots, I'll be questioning whether your motives are underhanded or not."

"I told you outside the bar, we'll take it one step at a time, Pay. And if it means we keep this platonic until you're ready to trust in us and give me a second chance, then we will."

"You want to try again?" Her heart moved to her throat, and swallowing was difficult around a mound of regret.

Goddess, please don't let it be the boots influencing him!

"I don't know. Maybe." He brushed his thumb over her lower lip. "Will you think less of me if I told you I was afraid?"

She shook her head. "What are you afraid of? Me?"

"Yes. What if I give you my whole heart and soul again, only to have you run? I won't survive it a second time," he admitted.

"I'm not sure I would either." But her words were drowned out by the commotion outside.

He cast a frowning glance over his shoulder, but didn't immediately respond.

"Go see, Lee. We can pick this up again."

Banging on the door interrupted whatever he intended to say, and he growled his frustration as he headed to answer his visitor's summons.

"Where in the fire and brimstone is my sister?"

"Elara?" Payton rushed forward, hugging her. "What are you doing here?"

"Tripp got to the bar, and it was pure chaos. With his help, we put them all to sleep."

"All of them?" Dailey asked, shrugging back into the coat he'd removed upon arrival. "For fuck's sake, Elara. Don't you know when to leave well enough alone?"

Payton bristled. "Don't speak to her that—"

An explosion rocked the cabin, and windows shattered, showering glass in every direction.

She dropped to the floor, dragging Elara with her and covering her sister's body with her own. Dailey piled on, attempting to shield them both. Three-inch shards, along with hundreds of smaller fragments, hung in midair as if frozen in time.

"Get. Off!" Elara ground out as she struggled to escape their impromptu huddle. Her cheeks were flushed, but her eyes, typically sparkling with light and happiness, were dark with annoyance. "I almost couldn't construct the protective bubble with you two smothering me."

"Bubble?" she and Dailey echoed.

Her sister waved an arm to indicate the space around them. A rolling shimmer highlighted various areas of the dome.

"How badass!" Payton breathed in wonder as she touched a finger to the inside wall. Other than a light zing, she felt nothing. "When did you learn to do this?"

"Tripp taught me. You could've joined our lessons if you'd have stuck around."

Her tone wasn't condemning, and her wording was very matter-of-fact. Yet Payton felt the sting. Perhaps it was the tightening of Dailey's mouth and the way he glanced down as he fought not to weigh in.

"What do you suppose was the source of the explosion?" she asked, redirecting everyone away from her.

Tripp stepped through the door on the tail end of her question. With a single encompassing glance, he waved a hand, collecting all the glass, and restored the windows to their original state.

"A meteor. Much larger this time," he replied. With a pointed look for Dailey, he said, "I took care of it, but you must numb your feelings or get a handle on your emotions."

"Yeah, I'm trying." Dailey smiled his regret at Elara. "I'm sorry. Payton was right. I should've tempered my aggravation and worry. Please accept my apology."

"For what it's worth, I'm sorry I cursed you," she replied. "You have to know it was all my fault, and Payton had nothing to do with it."

"And none of it was intentional," Tripp added with a loving smile for Elara followed by a glare at Payton's boots. "When we finally get those blasted things off your feet, I'm going to burn them."

"Not if our resident chaos gremlin, Hermes, has anything to say about it," Dailey said in disgust. "Rest assured, whenever I see him, I'm going to inform Cory of his whereabouts. He strikes me as a man with a score to settle."

"How did you know where to find us?" Dailey didn't mind their unannounced arrival, but he wasn't necessarily thrilled his conversation with Payton had been cut short. It seemed whenever they were making headway, they were interrupted. "And why are you here?"

"Hermes," Tripp replied.

"Goddess, I'm beginning to despise that man's name," he said feelingly. "Please continue."

"Apparently, when he was forced to flee the bar, his hold over Cory's customers broke. He was worried about Payton possibly being inundated with "amorous beaus" and sent us to subdue the crowd."

Elara nodded. "When we got to the bar, you'd just left. Tripp figured you'd come here first, since it was the farthest from town."

Dailey only recently obtained this place through a private holding company. After the purchase, he warded the entire property so his mother couldn't track him when he needed a respite from her managing behavior. Perhaps part of him viewed it as a potential oasis for Payton and him.

"How did you know about this cabin?" he asked Tripp.

"Oh, he knows everything," Elara declared with a proud-as-punch grin for her new fiancé.

"But my newest purchase was kept private on purpose, so the residents of Witchmere couldn't find me."

With no outward expression of guilt, the demigod shrugged. "I keep a dossier on all of Witchmere."

"Did you know Cory was a dragon?" Payton asked.

Her curiosity matched Dailey's. But the bigger question was why Tripp was keeping tabs on everyone.

"Yes. Corvack. He moved here from Drakoryth to start over."

"From?" he asked.

"Death," Tripp said succinctly. "I won't reveal any more of his reasons, but they seemed valid at the time he told me."

"Why spy on your neighbors?"

"An old habit derived from years of dodging my mother and trying to determine who she might use to find me." Pink dusted his cheekbones, and he cast a sheepish glance around as if suddenly uncomfortable with the topic. "But none of that matters, Cobb. We have a serious problem on our hands. Payton is a beacon in those blasted boots. If there's a person within a hundred yards of us, they'll come calling."

"Why is this happening?" she cried. "And how do I make it stop?"

Surprisingly, it was Elara who answered. "The boots amplify your feelings and magic, sister. From what I can tell, they use your worst insecurity, reverse it, and throw it out into the world."

"Reverse it," Dailey said softly. He considered what he knew about Payton and how it could be used against her. "You never feel good enough," he concluded aloud. "You believe no one could possibly want you for who you are."

She paled. "So now everyone wants me."

"That about sums it up," Tripp replied grimly. "You need protectors until we can clear this up."

"But who? If everyone I come in contact with wants to

boink me, who do I trust?" She frowned. "And why haven't you made a pass at me yet?"

"Having already been subjected to Hermes's special brand of magical shit, Elara and I are immune."

"So I am, too." Dailey winked at Payton. "I told you my desire to rip your clothes off was all me."

He chuckled as she flushed a becoming berry shade.

"I'm afraid you aren't," Tripp said. "You're still under the influence of the original curse."

"No, I'm not. I feel things again." He met Payton's hopeful gaze. "Love, protective, optimistic."

Regret welled in Elara's wide blue eyes. "It's not real, Dailey. That's also what we came to tell you."

Fear. Yeah, another emotion he hadn't felt in forever was coursing through him, prepared to override his ability to reason. He inhaled, attempting to shove it aside.

"Explain," he barked, wincing at the harshness of his demand. They didn't notice or, if they did, didn't care to call him on it.

Tripp kissed Elara's temple and urged her farther into the room. "Have a seat, flitter mouse. I'll conjure coffee for everyone." To Payton, he said, "Why don't you join her, while Dailey helps me?"

She looked like she was about to drop at any moment, and Dailey reached for her, only to have her wince and dodge him.

Crushed, he stepped back. He understood her reticence; how could he not? She believed he was under some stupid spell and not truly committed to her this time around. But she was wrong.

"We'll return in a moment," Tripp assured them, gesturing Dailey to follow him.

Walking away from Payton with her devastated expression felt impossible. The pull of her—Oh, Christ! He met Tripp's concerned gaze.

"You're right, aren't you? I'm still cursed, and like Payton, the spell has morphed, making me feel everything but amplified."

"Yes."

He glanced at her to see her reaction. The sight was gutting. Her eyes were filled with disappointment, and her pain was made evident by the shimmering tears she valiantly held at bay.

"It's okay, Dailey," she said, offering a tragic smile. "We'll find a way to break it."

But what did that mean? Would his re-emerging feelings for her go away again? Would they be back to square one, with him despising her and her fleeing from his condemnation?

"Payton—"

"Rein it in, okay? For now, don't think long term." Her smile, though shaky, widened. "We don't need an asteroid taking out Witchmere."

And wasn't that the crux of the matter? He alone had the ability to destroy the town, or quite possibly the entire planet if his rage got away from him again.

As mildly as he could, he said, "I'm going to kill Hermes."

Tripp shot him a commiserating look. "That's why he sent us."

CHAPTER THIRTEEN

Dailey didn't truly love her.

His forgiveness was all a result of an enchantment Payton had no way of removing.

Her chest ached, and the desire to have Witchmere in her rearview was growing exponentially with every painful inhale.

"Please stay calm, P." Elara clasped her hand, bringing it up to her cheek. "Please don't run away until we can resolve this."

"I wasn't planning on it," she lied. But her sister saw straight through her, as she always had. She glanced toward Tripp and Dailey over by the kitchen counter. "What do I do, El? I thought he forgave me and might be on his way to loving me again. But it's all an illusion."

Elara sandwiched Payton's face between her palms and leaned in with the intensity of someone hoping to make a point. "Listen to me. Dailey loves you. If he didn't, there would be nothing to magnify."

"But you and Tripp just said the boots amplified feelings in reverse. Meaning, deep down, he still hates me."

"No. You're misheard. The spell attached to him changed. It went from taking away his feelings to returning them with a vengeance. Meaning his love for you was already great. Now, he's ready to annihilate anyone his brain sees as a potential threat. With ever-increasing-sized meteors," she stressed. "All to protect you."

As Payton considered this new angle, the tightness in her chest lessened.

"When can I trust this to be over? How did you and Tripp resolve your issues?"

"Ours centered around commitment to one another. Maybe yours is the same."

Was it as simple as her sticking?

A stone at the tip of her shoe illuminated as her feet grew warm. "Uh, El, is this normal?"

"Yes. For every jewel that lights, you have a problem to solve."

"So just the one is good?" Optimism was slowly creeping in until Payton saw Elara scrunch her nose. "What?"

"It isn't a science. For me, one lit whenever I guessed another thing I needed to address. Parents, relationships, admitting my love for Tripp, acknowledging my fears."

"That's right! I'd forgotten." She attempted to recall their conversation. It had something to do with Elara's list of people she needed to speak to and settle the score.

The boots put on a full-blown light show—Vegas-level—then dimmed back to the single stone.

"Fucking great."

"What were you thinking about when the diamond lit?" Elara asked.

"Commitment. I... Wait! Diamond? I thought they were rhinestones."

"Girl, no! You have a king's ransom on your feet."

"Would you mind if I borrowed your fiancé as a bodyguard?" Though she sounded like she was kidding, she totally wasn't. The idea of strutting around in millions of dollars' worth of footwear was unnerving.

"Oh, we've formed an entire babysitting brigade." Elara's grin shouted self-congratulations for her own cleverness. "We'll use anyone not affected in round-the-clock shifts."

"So you and Tripp," she replied dryly.

"Verron and Hermes, too."

"Not Hermes. If I see that twatwaffle again, I'm going to separate his dick and balls from his body then drop them into the Mariana Trench."

Elara giggled, bless her heart, believing Payton wasn't serious. Clearly she didn't understand Payton's current level of fury with the Trickster.

The guys returned with a tray of coffee and sandwiches. Payton rose, allowing Tripp the spot beside Elara, then she sat on the opposite couch. Dailey joined her, but he left space between them, unlike the couple across from them.

The happy twosome were cuddled down, sharing a plate, with Tripp stealing all the chips and grinning between bites. They were perfect for each other. A year ago, Payton wasn't quite so sure, but their bond had strengthened. Where Elara was light, Tripp was dark. Looking at them, one would mistakenly believe he held all the power, but it was she who was the stronger of the two.

"You told me the boots required you to commit, but you once mentioned other issues with people that needed to be resolved," Payton said. "What were they *exactly*?"

Her sister frowned as she attempted to recall. "Mom and Dad were one. The abandonment, accepting our heritage. Finding out about Flo being our grandmother was another. The sense of betrayal was strong."

"But you have to understand, the spell attached to those magical menaces will not be the same for you, Payton," Tripp warned, causing her stomach to tighten. "You'll need to figure it out before Dailey creates a global-extinction event like with the non-avian dinosaurs."

"Not funny," Dailey said sourly.

"Not kidding," Tripp replied.

Payton inhaled deeply and lifted her chin to meet the challenge head-on. "Okay, we'll figure out the key problem. Dailey was right. For me, as hard as it is to admit, it's the feeling of not being good enough."

"And for me, it's the crushing failure I experience when I can't please everyone or keep them safe," Dailey said.

She glanced down, but only one stone was illuminated. "Did anyone catch what triggered it?"

"You did, which means he isn't being a hundred percent honest." Tripp gave him a pointed look. "Dig deeper."

"Maybe therapy with Harrison will help," Elara suggested with a bright smile and a pat on his shoulder. "It worked for you, right?"

The demigod's eyes danced with humor, and his tone was droll when he confirmed it had. In other words, it hadn't. Not really. Whatever conclusions Tripp had reached were primarily on his own.

"What about couples therapy?" Payton touched Dailey's hand. "We don't have to see Harrison; we can go to another doctor."

"Pay, our situation is unique," he hedged.

Her hope died. If he didn't want to work on their problems, there was nothing more she could do.

Turning to Tripp, she asked, "If I were to leave here, go far away, would Dailey still be affected?"

Dailey didn't give him time to answer. "What the fuck? This is precisely what I'm talking about, Payton. When things get hard, you bolt."

A second jewel lit.

And outside... a *FWOOOOOOOSH*, followed by a resounding crash.

"I need a sedative," he muttered.

"Not to say I told you so, but—"

He cut her a *don't-you-dare-say-it* look.

Compressing her lips, she nodded.

The need to escape was stronger than he'd ever experienced, and he had the fleeting thought that perhaps this was what Payton felt whenever a situation overwhelmed her.

Another diamond illuminated.

"What were each of you thinking?" Elara asked excitedly.

"I didn't want to piss him off again," Payton said with a wary side glance at him.

Was she afraid of him? His skin prickled, and his hands grew clammy as his sense of unease grew. "You don't piss me off. This entire nightmare does. Hermes should never have given you such a dangerous gift."

"But what thought ran through your mind prior to Payton's comment?" Tripp prodded.

He wasn't ready to confess, but he also knew complete honesty was paramount.

"I experienced an urge to get away, and wondered if the overwhelming need was what Payton felt whenever things got rough."

The light flickered before flaring brighter and returning to normal.

"Understanding her point of view is one of your lessons!" Elara's excitement was contagious.

For the longest of moments, Tripp watched him. "How do you feel about your mother?"

Dailey recoiled, and embarrassment for his visceral reaction heated his skin. "I'm not discussing my mother with any of you until I'm on elephant tranqs." To Payton, he said, "This isn't rejection. I just need to work through all of it in my head first. Besides, I see flames through the window. I should see about the damage."

She caught his hand when he stood. "Do you want us to add an emotion-numbing spell?"

Curbing his desire to swear half of outer space down upon them, he shook his head and dashed for the door.

Tripp followed him out.

"Please, can I get a damned minute alone, Nightshade?"

"You could, but two of us are better than one when it comes to extinguishing the forest fire." Tripp indicated the ridge behind him.

What looked to be an acre of his land was ablaze, and the

sinking sensation returned. Would his life ever be normal again?

As if the Gods were tuned in, two men appeared on the other side of the gravel driveway.

"I guess the cavalry has arrived," he muttered with a sigh. "Thank the Goddess they didn't bring Junior or I might throw myself under a falling tree."

"I feel your pain."

The only consolation was that Tripp didn't love having Hermes around any more than he did.

"Can we beat the hell out of him when the boots are finally off Payton's feet?"

The demigod's grin was pure evil, and promised retribution shone in his dark eyes. "I have a much better revenge in mind."

"Care to share? It might put me in a better mood."

"A taste of his own medicine."

Dailey considered what a serving of Karma might be. "You plan to gift him the boots next?" he asked with an incredulous laugh.

"Indeed." Tripp chuckled, and it was as menacing as his grin. "And I know just the Goddess to do it."

CHAPTER FOURTEEN

Payton jumped up the instant they left. "I can't just sit here like a lump on a log, El. I'll go insane in under an hour."

"Did you not hear anything we just discussed?" Elara set aside her sandwich and sighed. "You are giving in to panic again. Besides, if you go anywhere, you'll be running the gauntlet of horney men and women, all vying for your attention."

"Shit!"

In all her angst over Dailey, she'd forgotten she was a pork chop to hungry dogs everywhere.

Elara gave her a sickly smile. "On the bright side, at least you aren't causing earthquakes and volcanic explosions."

"Oh, and rocks burning up the atmosphere are so much better? We need Hermes," she concluded with a grimace.

"We do," her sister agreed. "Or at the very least, Tripp's mom, Brelenia."

"Why her?"

"Based on a conversation I overheard between Hermes and Tripp. I believe she's heavily involved in matchmaking."

"Why would she do this to *me*, though?" Payton asked. She couldn't recall meeting the woman.

"Do the deities ever need a reason to twist a person's life into a pretzel?"

Elara had a point. Likely, they rolled the dice and gambled on the outcome for fun, leaving the helpless humans to pick up the wreckage of their lives.

"Okay, go get—"

Hermes stepped through the door wearing a roguish grin.

"I really hate him," she muttered.

"It might help if he looked like a troll instead of a, well, *god*."

She did a double-take to make sure it was still her sister standing beside her and not Rowan. "Elara Elizabeth Hawthorne!" she hissed. "What would your new fiancé have to say?"

"My beauties signaled your need, love," Hermes said as he approached them. "What is it you'd request of me?"

"Oh, I don't know, let me think. Oh yeah, how about you get these damn things off my feet and—"

He pressed a finger to her lips, but it turned into the lightest of caresses. A frown tugged his brows together, and when his eyes met hers, there was confusion in the depths. It was as if his action disconcerted him.

She knocked his hand away. "What the hell, dude?"

"That shouldn't have happened," he said softly, his concern made evident by the way he backed away from her and stared at his hand.

"What? What happened?" she and Elara asked together.

"You must find a way to boost your self-confidence, Payton. If you don't, the boots will double down on the wanton enchantment. No one will be safe from the effects soon."

"What does that even mean?" she cried. Her trepidation was growing exponentially. "Are you saying you felt the pull just now?"

"Yes. And it's dangerous for a god to be attracted to a Titan."

"What about Tripp?" Elara asked, with a squeak high enough to summon mice.

"He's a demigod, not quite at full strength. But he, too, will succumb."

"But he and Elara... They... He can't..." Payton began dumbly. She faced her sister, who looked as horrified as she felt. "What do I do? Aren't we stronger together? Can we use our power to counteract all this BS?"

Ignoring her questions, Elara addressed him. "When this enchantment grows, and I sense it already has, the attraction won't just stop at her, will it? It will expand to everyone in every setting, suddenly feeling randy."

"It's possible."

"Possible or probable," Payton asked sharply.

"Probable." His expression was grim, and for once, he wasn't pretending or covering up his mischievous tendency. "The wantonness will spread, and every living thing will succumb, uncaring of commitments or connections. The need to procreate will consume everything."

"Get these off my feet, Hermes! Right now!"

"I can't, Payton. I want to, truly, but they have to run

their course before they can be removed." He sought support from Elara. "Tell her. You know. You wore them in many lifetimes."

"Yes, and they caused an insane amount of grief. Last year, Tripp and I were on the verge of taking out half of America." She rushed him and shoved his chest, sending him into the wall. "It was irresponsible of you and Brelenia to pull this stunt again. How many lives will you wreck with your stupid games, Hermes?"

Payton plopped into the chair, shaken to her core. "Is the same thing in store for Dailey and me? This destroying each other and the world over many lifetimes until we get it right? What if these increase his ability, and he creates a global event?" She met Hermes's regretful stare. "People will hump to death or die from a planet-extinction asteroid."

"Worrying about the future isn't dealing with the here and now," he said firmly. "Focus! Begin listing all the wonderful things about yourself, and repeat it as a mantra until you feel it. If you can't find it within you, have Dailey and Elara help. But trust them to tell you the truth, Payton. Believe in yourself. Believe people truly want you, and not in a mongrel-hump-your-leg way."

His desperation, combined with his words, struck her funny bone. She giggled. Then gave in to her amusement at his and Elara's shock. Madness numbed her mind to anything but their horrified expressions, and she doubled over, scarcely able to breathe, as tears streamed down her cheeks.

"The… visual…" she gasped. "People… humping others'… legs!"

Elara was the first to break, and a giggle erupted from

between her lips, followed by laughter until she, too, was bent in half, clutching her ribs.

Dailey entered to find the women hysterical and Hermes looking like he'd eaten a lime. His puckered expression seemed to send Elara and Payton further over the edge.

"What did we miss?" Tripp asked, delight in his tone as he watched them. There was a man who truly appreciated his woman enjoying herself, especially if it was at Hermes's expense.

Dailey had been like him once. Whenever he and Payton had gone out and she let loose, he'd sit back, relax, and relish the show. The pleasure he'd gained from knowing how much she enjoyed herself was immeasurable. Where had that couple gone? When had he begun putting the wants of the town and his mother above theirs?

A stone lit on her boots, and he was the only one to notice.

There was no denying what it represented—his recognizing he'd put her last when she should've been his number one priority.

Crossing to her, he squatted and clasped her hand. "Hey."

She sobered, watching him warily.

"I owe you the biggest fucking apology ever," he began. "I—"

Her lips parted, and her tongue darted out to wet them, distracting him.

What was he saying? Something about an apology…

Her cheeks grew flushed, and her curious gaze dropped

to his mouth. Once again, she licked her lips, the moisture causing them to glisten.

He craved a taste.

Just one, and then he'd remember what he'd been about to say.

Leaning forward, she met him halfway. They were inches from connecting when Hermes shouted. The words were unintelligible, irksome in their garbled delivery, and Dailey was too focused on Payton to care.

Hands grabbed him, rough and unrelenting, dragging him from his objective. He fought like a madman to get back to her. The need to be with her consumed him.

"Knock him the fuck out, Tripp!" Hermes shouted. "He's either going to bring down the heavens, or he's going to curse us all forever by partaking of the forbidden fruit!"

The mention of the latter snapped Dailey out of the bewitchment consuming him.

"What the hell are you talking about?" he asked, still half dazed.

The sisters were staring at his crotch in wide-eyed wonder. He dared a downward glance, then groaned his embarrassment.

What the actual fuck was happening? How had the promise of a stolen kiss sent him into such a state of arousal that he'd forgotten others were present?

"It's not you," Tripp said, as if reading his mind. "Her draw is stronger, I can feel it tugging at me. Hermes?"

"Yes. It's morphing into a whole other animal. Soon enough, we'll all be walking around with stiffies or hiding behind the shed to rub one out," Hermes replied grimly.

Never mind the fact that an ancient God used the term

"rub one out," the added visual was as disturbing as it was funny. Apparently Payton and Elara thought so, too, because they dissolved into laughter.

"I don't understand what this is all about, but you can let me go now." The instant they did, his attention was caught by the golden gleam of Payton's hair, positioned temptingly over her shoulder. Her come-hither smile beckoned him, and he was determined to fulfill her wishes.

He was unaware of moving until rough hands dragged him backward again.

"What the hell?" he snapped, ready to curse them to perdition.

"Stay calm," Tripp warned. "And please hear me when I say, you must leave this place. Payton's hold over you is growing, and it's taking all our magic to restrain you."

"She's always had a hold over me," he retorted. Seeing her concern, he smiled his adoration, no longer afraid to reveal how much he cared. "I love you."

"Although I believe you do, what you're experiencing in this moment is obsession, Cobb," Hermes stated in a low voice for his ears alone.

Outraged, Dailey renewed his struggle. "No! It's not obsess—"

The God clapped a hand over Dailey's mouth and shot a panicked glance Payton's way.

Following the man's sightline, he witnessed her expression crumple into dejection. He licked Hermes's palm, hoping to ick him into uncovering his mouth.

It worked.

"Payton," Dailey cried, his anguish at her pain hitting an all-time high. Fighting the two holding him, he strove to get to her. Sweat pooled at his armpits, and he became fevered with the need to comfort her. "It's okay, Wildfire, it will all be all right. I promise, my love."

But the more he spoke, the worse her upset became, until it forced him to shut up.

Elara wrapped her in a tight hug, rubbing a hand along her back. "He's high on magic, Pay. But he does love you. It's magnifying, remember?"

High? Yes, it was precisely how he was feeling. His mind was fuzzy, and a strange lethargy flowed through him, as if he'd been drugged. Yet he hadn't consumed anything since breakfast.

Which meant Payton was the source!

They stared at each other in horror, recognizing the problem at once. If he couldn't get close to her without succumbing to her seductive charms, they couldn't resolve their problems. And without that resolution, those boots weren't going anywhere until their world, quite literally, exploded.

CHAPTER FIFTEEN

Payton was on the verge of tears, but she'd be damned if she'd show it.

She loved Dailey. Those feelings hadn't disappeared since their parting, and this new development, where being near her triggered his destructive behavior or amorous thoughts not his own, was problematic. Yes, Elara was clinging to the belief that his love was the cause, but Payton knew better. She refused to have him consumed by feelings not his own.

"We need a plan," she said, determined to put an end to all of the madness. "Where can I go to isolate myself from others, and how do we stop this magic from escalating further?"

"Another realm?" Tripp asked, directing the question to Hermes. "Perhaps Vorren—"

"No!" Dailey snapped.

Plink-plink-plink.

Elara glanced up. "Is the roof on fire?"

Tripp cursed, but snuffed out the danger with a simple wave.

"Dailey, please control your anger." Payton rubbed her forehead, hoping to dispel the building migraine. "There is no reason for jealousy. Is Vorren stupid hot? Yes. Am I going to jump his bones? No. There will be no sexual escapades for me until these things are off my feet."

"Good." Hermes gave an approving nod. "It's best if you don't. The two of you engaging in sexual congress without resolving your issues will be catastrophic."

She froze. "How?"

Dailey jerked, whipping his head to the side to frown at Hermes. "You said, and I quote, 'He's either going to bring down the heavens, or he's going to curse us all forever by partaking of the forbidden fruit!' The first half I get, but what the hell does the last bit mean?"

Payton's heart thudded, and her anxiety spiked. Was she the forbidden fruit destined to curse them all forever?

With his skin a sickly pallor, Hermes grimaced.

"Tell them," Tripp ordered in a stern tone. "They deserve to know what's happening to them."

"I can sense the energy shift," the Trickster began. "As with Elara, the combination of your magic, the ever-changing power of the boots, and my Trickster influence has caused the original spell to become something greater."

"That cleared up exactly nothing," Dailey snapped.

"I believe what he's saying is the combination of all three is causing the enchantment to become a living, breathing beast," Payton said slowly. "I never felt wanted, and instead of giving me confidence, I'm now wanted by every living creature, except my family, correct?"

Hermes nodded.

"And Dailey, whose feelings were taken away, now has an overabundance of feelings he's finding difficult to control," she added.

"Yes."

"But both of those things are expanding by the minute. You fear that if we don't resolve our issues but give in to lust, it could forever damn us."

"Yes. I know I said you should stay in Witchmere, but it was to keep you and Dailey together."

"So you lied," she said flatly.

He scrunched his nose and shrugged. "Meh. I suppose you could say I stretched the truth a bit, but now it's no longer safe for you."

"What's to stop this from spreading if I go to another realm with Vorren? What if the people there are consumed? Also, did he agree to this?"

"He's right outside. You can ask him yourself." Hermes gestured toward the window.

"You didn't answer me," she stated coolly with a raised brow.

"The truth is, I don't know. I don't think it will follow you, but I cannot be sure."

"Then I'll stay here on earth." The last place she wanted to be was with a kingdom of creatures she didn't know jack-shit about. She turned to Tripp. "Can you find me a deserted island, or at least create one with amenities?"

"Yes."

"Thanks."

Elara raised her hand. "Um, I hate to be the blight on this plan of yours, but how will you resolve your issues if you are alone on an island? Neither of you will be able to work through your issues."

"She's right." Tripp smiled at her like she was the brightest of pupils.

Payton tamped down her envy, fearing she'd never have a relationship as beautiful as theirs. Her gaze drifted to Dailey, who watched her closely.

"What do you think, Lee? You're the other half of this, too."

He crossed to the window, his gaze following the movement outside. "What if we stay here, you and I?"

"That's unwise—"

He cut Hermes off with a look.

"I get it. But the dragon can stay to keep the others at bay and play catcher to my incoming meteors. We can see if Cory will join him. Between the two of them, I feel they could fend off the more persistent lovelorn vying for Payton's hand."

Tripp narrowed his eyes in contemplation. "Go on."

"Additionally, with all of us, we can come up with a spell to keep Payton and me apart. Possibly electrocute me if I go near her."

"Lee!"

Dailey cast her a lopsided grin. "Trust me, I'm not into self-punishment, but if it helps prevent a widespread calamity, then I'll do it."

"How does any of this resolve the problem?" she asked.

"You and I will be sequestered here to work through our issues."

"And if we don't?"

His expression was steely. "We will. We don't have a choice."

Shy of him shipping his mother to Siberia, she couldn't see them resolving diddly squat. But she didn't voice it aloud. If he favored positivity, who was she to naysay him? She'd bolster his optimism if she could.

"I'm not sure I'm comfortable with this scenario," Elara said, casting a worried glance between them. "What if the electric-fence idea fails?"

Dailey didn't have an answer. He'd fallen back on his original hair-brained idea to abduct Payton and keep her here until she removed the spell. Yet like the boots, his objective was changing. Mainly because his emotions were no longer numb, and his love for her had been rekindled.

His only fear? He couldn't trust it.

And Payton knew it, too.

He could see it in her eyes, the wariness, the inability to believe herself worthy of his devotion. If he were smart, he'd second her remote-island suggestion, but her absence would kill him. A life without her would finish him for good this time around.

"Pay? What is it you want?" he asked softly.

A stone lit on the left boot.

Well, at least he was making progress by considering her feelings, right?

Another diamond flared bright.

Jesus! Was it really so simple?

"What are you thinking?" she asked. With her head tilted in curious confusion and her eyes filled with caution, she appeared vulnerable. Dailey wanted so desperately to hold her, but he couldn't risk it until they had a failsafe in place.

"About how much you should have a voice in all of this," he replied. "About how I need to make things right and provide a safe space for you to be yourself without outside influences."

Two more jewels came to life.

"You seem to be working through your half of things," she said.

Her smile was bittersweet, and for the life of him, he couldn't grasp why she was so freaking sad.

"We'll work through them together, Wildfire," he promised.

Elara wrapped an arm around her sister's waist. "You two may be further along than Tripp and me. I'm feeling good about your chances this lifetime."

Dailey barked a laugh, startling himself and the others. Unfortunately for him, Payton didn't find it as humorous.

"What's so funny?" she demanded.

Her fire was a sight to behold, and he grinned.

Balling her fists, she charged, only to be caught by Tripp and Elara. The former released her as if burned, paled, and backed up.

"Hermes, she's stronger."

"I know. I feel it, too."

The grim response didn't bode well, and Dailey's humor fled.

"Then let's ward the house, and protect her from everyone, me included," he said.

"This may take more firepower than two compromised gods," Hermes replied. For the span of a few heartbeats, he stared at Payton, then he snapped his fingers. "I've got it. The gargoyles!"

"What about them?" he asked.

Tripp grinned. "Of course!" Withdrawing his phone, he made a call. "Archer, I need a favor." They all remained quiet as he relayed the problem to Archer Roche, Witchmere's ancient guardian. "How many of your clan can you rally to protect Payton?" He glanced at the occupants of the room. "Just Dailey and Payton with Cory and his brother-in-law, Vorren." Tripp paused to listen. "Dragons. And yes, I know you are on separate sides of the divide, but—"

The demigod hung his head and sighed.

Dailey's stomach tightened, fearing the worst. If the rumor was true, a war might break out between the gargoyles and dragons. As Tripp had hinted at in his conversation, the two opposing factions were in a centuries-old feud. Of course, Dailey had never given it much credence, since he'd never encountered the winged menaces before. Or he hadn't believed he had until learning Cory was one earlier.

"Archer's been to *The Winking Wyvern*, hadn't he?" Payton asked in a hushed voice.

To a one, the rest of them shrugged.

Dailey couldn't recall Archer ever setting foot in the bar, which in itself was odd. His unique ability allowed him to remember everything. But in all the time he'd known the man— it had been his entire life—he'd never seen him enter the establishment. Had the guardian somehow known what Cory was?

Tripp's tone changed. "You are the protector of Witchmere, Roche. Do your damned job!"

Thunder boomed, rattling the windows, and dark clouds rolled in, casting shadows over the room.

"You dare—"

Elara snatched the phone. "Archer? Elara, here. Can you tell me what it would take for you and your clan to help my sister and Dailey?" As she listened, she strong-armed Tripp, playing keep-away with his device. She did, however, put it on speaker.

"… I'd like to help out, Elara. But the best I can offer is to come out myself. I cannot ask my brethren to set aside their grievances."

"What if Vorren went back to his realm?" Dailey asked. "You've co-existed with Cory until now."

"If the prince returns home, then yes," Archer agreed. "I will call my brother, Valken, to bring a small army."

Payton's brows shot up. "You have a brother?"

His raspy chuckle filled the air. "Do you believe I was hatched, like those devil dragons?"

"I've never given it much thought," she admitted.

"I will be there as soon as I can contact the others. I will require at least one to watch over the residents and another for the tourists."

"Two to do your job?" Dailey asked with a laugh, striving to keep it light.

"Something like that," Archer replied dryly. "Can you survive an hour or two until I can pull Cecil and Greer from Seattle?"

"We'll make do," Tripp assured him. "And Roche? Thank you."

"You can thank me by ousting Prince Vorren and his men."

Dailey's jaw dropped. "Men? What men?"

"Drakoryth royalty doesn't go anywhere without their guards, Cobb," Archer explained. "If you didn't see them, it's because they've shielded themselves."

"How? A cloaking spell?" Elara asked.

Invisible visitors didn't sit well with Dailey. They played by a specific set of rules in Witchmere. All magical visitors had to announce themselves. Not only didn't Vorren do that, but he failed to alert them of his personal guard.

"Their scales are the source of their magic," Hermes explained. "They use them for camouflage, blending with their surroundings at half use, and complete invisibility when they are in full stealth mode."

"No wonder Archer is angry," Payton said, sidling up to him. "What—oh!"

The fragrance of her skin teased him, and Dailey leaned in to run his nose along the column of her neck, inhaling deeply.

"You smell divine," he whispered, touching his lips to her jaw. "I—"

She shoved him, sending him crashing into the door.

The knock to his head helped.

Mouth compressed into a thin line, she glared.

"I'm sorry, Pay." True shame washed over him. His inability to control himself was terrifying.

Without breaking eye contact, she raised her voice and asked, "Archer, are you immune to Trickster magic?"

CHAPTER SIXTEEN

Indeed, Archer was.

The reason Hermes suggested Witchmere's guardian was simple. Gargoyles were made of the earth and not subjected to the whims of the Gods.

Or not usually, anyway. There were a few rare cases. Steps could be taken to protect them from Payton's seductive vibe, and Hermes would do whatever was necessary to help his star-crossed charges.

Why the devil had he let Brelenia talk him into another project? Because he was a sucker for love. He hadn't always been. But since meeting and falling for Storm Bringer, Hermes had softened toward romance. Granted, Stormy hadn't. She was still furious with him after all these years. Yet, if he could help her sister, as he had with Elara, he might sway her—eventually.

His biggest concern? Payton's pull. Sure, she was sexy, and before Hermes realized her connection to Stormy, he may have entertained the notion of becoming lovers. Then he encountered his love again. Upon seeing how accepting she was of Elara, how willing she was to help her transition into her nymph-Titan self, he was forced to acknowledge he didn't want another.

Only her.

His Stormy.

She was as volatile as her name, and he was down for it.

But even Hermes wasn't immune to the boots anymore. They had gone rogue, becoming strong enough to snare anyone alive. Maybe dead, but hopefully those less fortunate souls would stay buried. It would take the whole gargoyle crew working overtime to defend themselves from Payton's new *eau de tap that* pheromone.

"I will ensure Vorren returns to his realm, Roche," Hermes promised.

"You can't." Payton shook her head. "Dragon Daddy's on a mission to find future babies. He was pretty fierce when he first landed. I wouldn't bet on anyone's chances if they try to stop his easter egg hunt."

"Payton's right," Dailey said. "There's no way he's leaving without his 'children.'"

"I'll be there as soon as my clan arrives," Archer said, voice tight. "Vorren can stay, but his henchmen go."

"Consider it done," Tripp assured him.

Hermes headed outside, leaving the others to handle arrangements with the gargoyle laird. He was halfway to Vorren when Dailey stepped in front of him.

"Are we risking a full-scale war, Hermes?"

"I don't know, Law Dog," he answered honestly. He'd been unable to resist the nickname and smothered a grin when Dailey scowled. "The gravel statues and pyromaniac lizards have been sworn enemies since the dawn of civilization. They were forged from opposing sources, fire and stone. After a boundary-breaking betrayal shattered their ancient pact, hell broke loose, ending whatever peace they'd maintained prior."

"What betrayal?" Dailey asked, as they resumed walking.

"A reckless youth decided he wanted the loot sealed inside a sacred tomb. The guardian didn't appreciate the intrusion. Some believe he overreacted when he ripped off the dragon's wings and had them stitched to his own body, using an enchanted thread."

Dailey jerked to a halt. "Are you fucking serious? They can do that?"

"Technically, yes. The idiot faced his partner in crime, prepared to thank her. Unfortunately for him, he forgot who he was dealing with. When he met Medusa's eyes, he was turned to stone."

"But they're already stone. That's part of their makeup and lore," he argued.

"No, not then it wasn't. Gargoyles were once flesh and bone, no different than you. Their power, however, is interwoven equally throughout the entire species. A shared magic, if you will. Medusa's curse spread through their bloodlines, binding them all to the crypts, churches, and buildings they once guarded."

Dailey blew out a breath. "Well, we know they can shift, so how did their ability come about?"

"There were those who petitioned the Gods for a reversal, arguing the creatures were essential in protecting their holy sites and castles. Without their guardians, the dragons were stealing their treasures, claiming their women, and eating their livestock. A few of the bolder ones commandeered fortresses or manor homes for their own."

"It must've worked. Archer can change at will."

"Yes, to a point. But every gargoyle must spend a minimum of twelve hours per day in their monolithic form. They can never be released completely. This is why there are multiple gargoyles on the richer estates. They take turns securing the property."

Vorren didn't bother climbing to his feet as they approached, and he continued using the blade of his pocketknife to scrape beneath his nails.

"Where did you get the knife?" Dailey asked, appearing disconcerted.

"Corvack. He remembers my superior throwing skill and feels it would be useful for me to have many weapons."

Brows reaching his hairline, the law dog shook his head. "Dare I ask where you've stored them?"

Vorren shot him a mocking grin, to which Dailey rolled his eyes.

"Yeah, never mind."

"I was never going to mind," Vorren replied with a dismissive shrug and focused on Hermes. "What is it you seek, Trickster? You are here for a reason, and probably not a good one."

"The Titan's curse is growing stronger—" he began.

The dragon prince snorted. "No thanks to your wicked magic."

"—and she needs defenders against the townspeople, as you are aware," Hermes concluded.

"Is this not why I am here? To kill your villagers when they arrive with their pitched forks?"

"There will be no killing of villagers. And it's pitchforks," Dailey corrected.

"No, he literally means pitched forks. It's a dragon euphemism for hard cocks," Hermes said, sighing heavily. "Vorren, we don't want you to kill the villa—er, townspeople. Most are decent, however simple they've become under the spell's influence."

"Yes, your foolish magic." The dragon prince rose and crossed his arms. "You will never learn not to meddle, Trickster."

"Probably not," Hermes agreed. "But there are gargoyles on the way and—"

Vorren spat at their feet, and the fury in his eyes said he was one huff away from lighting them up. "You dare? I will not be in the presence of those curs!"

The arrogance in his tone spoke of his lineage, as did the proud stance. At his full height of six-and-a-half feet, with shoulders wide enough to block the sun, the dragon appeared as formidable as Hermes knew him to be.

"It will be one—Archer—and he has agreed to a truce for Payton's benefit, but only if your men leave," Dailey said.

Vorren turned his fiery gaze on him. "You were not addressed, Law Dog. I am speaking to your devious friend."

Whether it was the officer in Dailey or his ego, Hermes couldn't begin to say, but the man's back went ramrod straight, and he stepped into the dragon prince's space.

"You're not a ruler here, Vorren. You're nothing more than an overgrown pyromaniac lizard with an attitude, and you certainly don't call the shots in my town."

"Pyromaniac lizard," Vorren said silkily, his eyes narrowing.

Hermes beamed and slapped Dailey on the back. "Our Law Dog here is a fast learner. He got that particularly fine insult from me." If he could deflect the dragon's rage to himself, his love-lorn charge had a better chance of survival and fulfilling the boots' demands, so the rest of the world survived.

"Incoming!" Tripp shouted from behind them.

FWOOOOOOOSH—

Hermes glanced up and swallowed hard. The meteorite above them was the largest yet. Without pausing to consider, he froze time.

Vorren shifted and glanced upward, but his movements were slow, similar to a person running through water. Hermes checked Tripp's response, wondering if he, too, had registered the dragon's ability to push through a god's magic.

His dark frown attested to the fact that he had.

"Free him to destroy the threat, Hermes," Tripp ordered.

The instant he did, Vorren half-shifted, as only royals of his realm could. His wings unfurled, wider than the expanse of the cabin, and he launched himself skyward from a dead stop. A single, forceful flap of those iridescent appendages bent trees under its tropical-storm strength winds. The second beat kicked up debris into the faces of those present, and Hermes quickly redirected it from those on terra firma.

Vorren's hands, now larger than a normal human's, sprouted talons, allowing him to grip the flaming rock. And, like an All-Star basketball player, he palmed the meteor and landed with grace, as if touching down from a slam dunk. Meeting Hermes's gaze, he said, "Unfreeze him."

Since Dailey was the only one still locked in place, there was little doubt about who the dragon prince referred to.

"If you intend to brain him with the rock, I'll have to object," he said, crossing his arms to show he meant business.

Tripp shielded Dailey by stepping in front of him. "Yes, no killing the mortals, Highness."

"I shall not kill him, but I am not beyond a physical display of strength. He should know who it is he insults."

Hermes shook his head as Tripp sighed and shifted away. "He won't be moved," he said.

Tripp nodded his agreement. "Likely, he'll double down on his rules for your visit."

Vorren lifted a brow, happy to wait them out.

"Fine." With a snap of his fingers, he reset time, then pointed behind Dailey when the man's face scrunched in his confusion. "There."

The instant the officer's gaze touched on him, the dragon prince pulverized the rock. Though he paled, Dailey squared his shoulders and stalked forward. "Another meteor." His tone was measured, face neutral. "It appears I must offer my thanks once again for your timely actions, Vorren."

"It was heading for me," the dragon prince retorted. "You tried to harm me with your sky stones!"

"Not on purpose." Dailey gestured to Hermes with his thumb. "You can blame that fucker."

After a long, measuring look, Vorren retracted his claws, dusted off his hands, and held one out. "Your bravery is noted, as is your wisdom of who the true culprit in your drama is. We shall become friends, you and I."

Dailey opened his mouth, but closed it just as quickly. Accepting the overture, he shook hands. "At the very least, friendly acquaintances."

Mouth twitching, as if fighting a grin, Vorren nodded and turned to Hermes. "I will require none of my detail to remain if you three shall vouch for the gargoyle. But if he betrays the truce, I will burn your village to the ground with all your people inside. Understood?"

"There is no need to threaten them, brother-mine."

Shimmering light encircled their group, as one by one, a small hoard of dragon guards appeared. There were ten in all, with the largest dressed all in black. He grinned in the face of Dailey's shock.

"You did not feel us? This is good," the man said.

The weighty stench of sulfur filled the air around them, and Dailey, unprepared, gagged.

"I suspected you were around, but not this close." His free hand fell to his belt, and Hermes suspected it was an old habit when he felt threatened or needed to resume control of a sticky situation. Too bad the arm covering his mouth and nose ruined his big-man-on-campass look.

"I present my half-brother, Nazek," Vorren said, ignoring Dailey's building tension and the offending smell. "Do not expect too much from him. He was dropped on his head at birth and is slower than most."

Nazek barked a laugh. "Yes, I am all brawn, no brain."

He was charming and relaxed, whereas his princely half-brother was haughty and rigid. Hermes attributed the difference to their stations in life. Vorren carried a burden he didn't wish to, and Nazek was free to be himself, without the weight of expectations or crowns.

"We've met." Tripp shot Nazek a grin. "It is good to see you again, my friend."

"And you, Nightshade." Turning to the other men, he said, "You shall return to Drakoryth."

To a one, the security detail protested. "King Rhagorr will disembowel us should we leave Prince Vorren unprotected."

"You aren't," Vorren said succinctly. "Nazek will stay. He, along with these gods, will ensure my safety."

Archer touched down on those words. Two gargoyles flanked him, and every dragon in the clearing went still.

Dailey hung his head. "Fuck."

CHAPTER SEVENTEEN

"None of that," Nazek chided, annoyingly cheerful. He flicked a glance toward the stony trio, his gaze lingering on the female's strikingly beautiful face before frowning and dismissing her with a slight shake of his head. "This party's heavy enough. No need to pile on." With a mocking grin aimed at Archer, he added, "Or is it pile up? Which one do you stoneheads prefer?"

Dailey was ready to spit nails. He could only imagine how annoyed Witchmere's protector must be. Stepping between the sworn enemies, he held out his hand. "Thanks for coming, Roche. I really appreciate it, and I know Payton does, too."

"They were supposed to be gone, Cobb," Archer replied tersely. "This is beginning to feel like a setup."

"No! No setup here. Besides, you're earlier than you stated you'd be." Exhaling a weary sigh, he said, "You know me, man. We've worked together to protect our town. And now, we need to again. Those fucking boots are on Payton's feet."

Archer scowled. "I will not put my clan in danger from another volcanic threat."

"Don't worry," Nazek said. "Lava flows right over rocks. You'll only be trapped for a short while. Say a millennium or so?"

"Can you kindly shut the fuck up?" Dailey snapped.

Vorren stepped between them. "If you cannot hold your tongue, you will go with the guards back to Drakoryth, brother-mine. And you can explain your behavior to our father and tell him that's why I sent you away."

With an exaggerated eye roll and a mimed lip-zip, Nazek stepped back, resting a shoulder against the large maple where Dailey and Hermes first came upon Vorren. Once again, his gaze drifted to the female.

"Vorren, please send your men away," Tripp said, careful to remain neutral and polite. "Time is running short."

After receiving a nod from their Prince, nine dragons took flight, eclipsing the sun for a moment before disappearing behind a cloud.

The gargoyle to Archer's left grinned evilly, balling his fists. "Foolish fucker—"

In a blinding move, the woman struck his throat and threw him to the ground. Standing over him with a foot resting on the troublemaker's chest, she growled low and fierce enough to cause the hair on Dailey's neck to stand at attention.

"You will not disrespect our family, Cecil," she said. "The laird has put his trust in us to keep the peace."

Archer placed a hand on her shoulder, and surprise of

surprises, Nazek straightened from the tree, with a scowl forming on his face.

"Do not touch her." The roar was aggressive and promised immediate retaliation should the command be disobeyed.

"Fuck," Dailey, Hermes, Tripp, and Vorren chorused, as Archer's already formidable build doubled in size.

"Did you know he could Hulk out like that?" Dailey asked Tripp in an aside.

"In theory, yes."

"What is happening? Why is your brother sprouting claws, and how the fuck do we stop him?" he asked Vorren, who was staring at Nazek like he was a new species.

"His dragon is treating her like she's his bonded mate," the prince replied, sounding somewhat awed. "Urge your friend to stand down, and do it now," he said urgently. "If Nazek has imprinted, he will kill first and ask questions later."

Hermes and Tripp took on the chore of calming Archer, while Vorren addressed his brother. But the smartest play was to remove the woman from the mix.

"Greer? Right?" Dailey gave her a professional smile at her wary nod. "Greer, would you be so kind as to check on Payton and Elara? They're probably wondering what's taking us so long."

Her gaze flicked to Nazek, and a deeper, elemental emotion flared between them. She couldn't seem to tear her eyes away.

"Go, woman," the dragon commanded.

Only then did her will return, and with a confused look for Archer, she hurried away.

"Ah, young love, am I right?" Hermes quipped with a slap on Tripp's back. "Who knew we'd play matchmaker to so many?"

"You're a fucking idiot," Tripp muttered with a shove to his cousin's chest. "Clean up your fucking mess, and don't start World War III."

"The small man sent me in here to check on you."

Payton pivoted toward the open doorway, taking in the redheaded bombshell with the Amazonian stature with her Slavic-sounding accent. "And you are?"

"Greer."

"Who is the small man?" Elara asked with an adorable frown.

"The non-god."

Payton snorted. Oh, Dailey would just *love* to be known as "the small man."

Unfortunately, Elara didn't look any less confused.

"She means Dailey," Payton said. "But I wouldn't call him small by any means," she couldn't resist adding.

Humor lit Greer's eyes when Elara choked on her drink.

"We just transitioned to wine." Payton waved toward the open bottle. "Care to share?"

"Yes," Greer said feelingly, casting a glance toward the hill where the men were gathered. After she was seated, with glass in hand, she asked, "What can you tell me about the smart-mouthed dragon?"

"Vorren?"

"No, his brother."

"His brother?" Elara and Payton parroted, sharing a surprised look.

They immediately popped up and pressed their noses the window. Sure enough, there was a beast of a man with similar coloring to that of Vorren. And like the prince, he wore his thick, wavy hair to his shoulders. The only thing missing was the silver streak.

"Nice eye candy, no?" Greer grinned before draining half her wine.

"The entire crew or the brother?" Payton asked dryly.

The other woman laughed. "I'll leave that to you to decide."

"So, I'm assuming you arrived with Archer, since he mentioned you and someone named Cecil earlier. You're a female gargoyle? I didn't realize they existed."

"We are few, but we do indeed exist, as I'm living proof." Greer swept a hand through the air, indicating her body. "There are four in total."

Her tone indicated she didn't care to speak of it, so Payton let it go. "You watch over Seattle?"

"At times, yes. Mostly, I travel, guarding rare-treasure events. Currently, the museum is hosting *The Lost Riches of the Sunken Citadel.*"

"I've read about that. A three-ship flotilla, carrying butt-loads of gold and jewels, was lost at sea. It's only been in recent years that proof of its existence emerged. Previously, it was believed to be an old wives' tale because no one could find documented proof of the manifests." Elara's eyes widened. "Isn't it like a billion-dollar event?"

"One point seven, to be exact," Greer replied without

missing a beat. "The gala is a single-night event, but the display will be year-long."

"How exciting! Payton, don't you find it exciting?"

"Considering your friend is wearing boots in the millions, she may not be as impressed as you." Greer shot her a sardonic smile.

Payton clasped Elara's hand. "Actually, we're sisters. We each take after the other parent."

A subtle hint of longing flashed in Greer's golden-brown eyes.

"You have no family?" she asked the gargoyle.

"Not in the truest sense. But we are all a clan of sorts. Archer is the oldest, and as such, became the laird."

"So no siblings?"

"Not a one," Greer said with a careless toast. "But cheers to that. It keeps the drama low."

"We don't have drama," Elara protested.

"El. Come on. We accidentally cursed Dailey, just found out last year Flo was our Gran and we're Titan-nymph hybrids."

"Okay, so there is that." She popped a grape and shrugged. "But at least we get along."

"When it counts."

"I would like sisters such as you," Greer blurted. "To be close to another female. To speak of... things. Confessions."

Her loneliness was great, and it didn't take an empath to see or hear it.

Payton leaned forward and refilled her glass, topping off Elara's and her own in the process. "We will be your sisters. Family doesn't always have to be blood."

Surprise flared on Greer's arrestingly beautiful face. "You would include me? But you don't know me."

"You are here to protect me, a person *you* don't know, and that tells me you've got a good heart."

"To sisterhood!" Elara said brightly, lifting her glass.

"To sisterhood!" Greer and Payton chorused.

Dailey entered, and his gaze landed on them. His smile flashed an instant before his eyes glazed over and his jaw slackened.

"What is wrong with him?" Greer asked, rising to her feet and stepping in front of them.

"My seductive powers must be growing again."

"That's not the only thing," Elara said, pointedly looking at Dailey's crotch.

Passion clouded his visage, and he strode forward, only to be blocked by Greer.

"I must—"

She didn't let him finish. "Get the fuck out."

"No, you don't understand." His gaze locked with Payton's. "I love you, Wildfire."

"Keep it in your pants, Romeo," Greer growled, blocking him with an extended arm and causing them all to gape in wonder at her strength when he couldn't push her out of his way.

What none of them expected was for him to disappear in a blink, pop up beside Payton, and fold her within his embrace.

"She's mine!"

She didn't have time to consider what his new possessiveness meant. Her cells warmed to burning, and right when she believed she couldn't take a second more, they arrived on a remote stretch of beach. A quick static swept along her body, a whispered warning, fading before she could register the meaning.

"Where the hell are we?" she demanded.

His grin was roguish as he stripped off his shirt. "Where no one will find us."

"Dailey, this isn't funny."

He toed off his shoes, and his fingers fell to his belt. "Who's kidding?"

"You and I can't—"

His jeans landed in a heap at his feet, leaving him bare assed with his dick pointing skyward.

"… Uh, can't…"

Her mind went blank the second he touched himself, and her body responded with a rush of heat. What the fuck had she been about to say?

"I intend to make love to you, Payton." His voice, husky and filled with desire, answered a driving need inside her. "Show me you want me as much as I want you."

With a snap of her fingers, she was as naked except for her footwear, which turned into sex-kitten slide-ons. Not practical for beachwear, but she wasn't getting them off anytime soon.

Dailey didn't seem to mind as he conjured a blanket, swept her up in his arms, and gently laid her down. His touch was as tender as his gaze but still hot enough to fan the flames inside her.

"Lee," she moaned as he found her sweet spot.

He captured her mouth in a drugging kiss, as he pleasured her, and when he tasted his way down her neck… her chest, pausing to suckle… then downward still, until his tongue on her core became the only thing that existed, Payton thought she'd died and gone to heaven. He inserted one finger, testing and stretching her to accept his second, all the while working his mouth magic. Gripping his hair, she pressed him closer and released ragged little pants between chants of "Yes!"

Light exploded behind her eyes, and the pleasure sweeping her body was next-level. Her feet tingled, and she curled her toes, bringing her knees up and rocking upward to extend the orgasm wave. Dailey indulged her, continuing to pump and lick, as if her prolonged pleasure was his only task in life.

A second explosion rocked her, and her body burned like never before.

It belatedly occurred to her that something was wrong.

Lifting her arms, she rotated her hands back and forth, stunned by the sparkling glow infusing her skin.

"Uh, Lee?"

When he glanced up, his expression was a promising blend of smugness and promise. But the instant he registered her illuminated skin, his reason seemed to kick back in.

"Oh, shit."

"'Oh, shit' is right," answered a tightly clipped female voice. "Get off her, you animal. My daughter needs the restorative powers of the water."

CHAPTER EIGHTEEN

"Mother!"

In her embarrassed surprise, Payton gripped Dailey's head, smothering his face against her mound to shield herself. His breath was hot against her sensitive folds, making her shudder, and his strangled voice was lost to the pounding in her ears. No matter how old one is, being caught in a compromising position by their parent is totally mortifying.

Pink tinged Mae Hawthorne's fair cheeks, but her China-blue eyes held amusement as they lingered on Dailey's perfect, sculpted ass. "Don't be embarrassed, darling. A healthy sex drive is natural for those from our bloodline. But you're running on empty, and you need to recharge. The ocean will help you with that."

Releasing him with a light shove, Payton snapped her fingers and clad herself in an airy robe.

His passionate protest drew her attention back to him.

His seductive gaze hypnotized her as the air around them grew thick with his desire.

"None of that!" Her mother clapped, and the sharp noise pulled Payton's head back around. "Your nymph is out of control, and if you don't reel it in, you two will literally hump to death."

Before a protest could form on Payton's lips, Mae pulled from her elemental source. Droplets rose from the sea and created a sigil in the space between Dailey and them. The symbol flared brightly, sizzling as it worked in accordance with the spell's design.

"Hm. The Trickster's magic is terribly strong, isn't it?" she murmured.

Flattening her palm, she held the existing enchantment in place, then sketched another with her opposite hand. Similar in design, the lines lit and crackled, like a flame along a dynamite fuse as it raced for the explosive. A wall of water rose from the sea, creating a thin barrier between Dailey and Payton. But the height and width made it impossible to breach.

It struck her that she was woefully unprepared to utilize her new Titan abilities. When all this mess with the Trickster was behind them, Payton intended to train.

"There, that should hold him for a few minutes," Mae said, her tone stating her satisfaction. She dusted off her palms. "Now, let's get down to business."

The lust-fog clouding Payton's mind dissipated, leaving her horrified, not only by being caught *in flagrante delicto* but also because they'd lost control, knowing the consequence of their actions should they have sex. What was it about being close to him that triggered her reckless behavior?

"Can't he walk through it?" Payton asked.

"No. Though liquid, it's solid. You can, however, toss him his clothes."

She did, marveling at how easily they passed through to the other side. "Can I cross it?"

"Yes, but I wouldn't recommend it, or my spell will be for naught."

With a heavy sigh, she faced her mother. "What's all this about?"

"Your skin is too dry, and your heat signature is high," Mae said gently. "Come. Let us soak a bit to rejuvenate."

"I do feel hotter than normal. I assumed it was the sun and, well, Dailey's um…" Her cheeks warmed until her face felt like it would combust at any moment. No amount of water was cooling her down. Chernobyl had nothing on her!

"I'm certain his ministrations helped, but I believe you're transitioning, as Elara did. The enchantment contained within the footwear is causing your power to develop faster than normal."

"Wonderful. Is there an underwater lair for people like us to cool off?" she asked dryly.

Her mother's smile suggested Payton's humor hadn't gone unnoticed. "There is, right off the coast of my home, but you refused to visit."

"Truly?" Payton blatantly disregarded her mother's underlying hurt. She wasn't the one who abandoned her parents; it was the other way around. "Like an Atlantis or something?"

"Or something," her mother agreed, holding out her hand. "Would you like to go there, or use the ocean here?"

On the other side of the wall, Dailey seemed to regain

his wits and drew on his underwear. His expression screamed that he wasn't happy about the interruption. Whether self-directed or at the interruption, Payton couldn't say, but she was feeling the exact same way. At least she'd received some satisfaction; he'd be suffering with blue balls soon.

"How did you know about all this?" she asked as they strolled to the water's edge.

"After Elara's incident, Storm Bringer contacted your father and suggested creating an early warning system for when your body went through the change. She didn't want you to suffer as your sister did."

"Why did no one tell me?" Although she didn't mind the help, it was annoying that no one thought to include her. "I'm a grown adult, able to judge when something is off inside."

Mae compressed her lips, then blew out a breath. "Darling, I hate to be the one to point this out, but you didn't know. That's why I'm here. You are reaching the red alert stage."

"Well, maybe the next time you and Father decide to procreate, you should think about informing your children what they are," Payton snapped. "It would've been nice to grow into our power instead of having it hit us like a ton of bricks."

"You'll feel better when you cool off, dear."

Would she?

Doubtful.

Her parents had disappeared at a formative time in her and Elara's lives, leaving them bobbing like corks in an endless sea of the unknown and unwanted. Her hurt wasn't going away overnight because they happened to show up now to take responsibility where they hadn't before.

The waves lapped against her calves, and as she walked farther out, her shoes changed to flippers. She had to smile. Hermes, bastard that he was, had thought of every footwear contingency.

On the other side of the wall, Dailey stalked her. Similar to a caged tiger pacing its enclosure, looking for a way to get to the tasty morsel on the other side.

She shivered.

"I wish you still loved me," she whispered. Hell, she wished anyone besides Elara and Rowan cared about her. Truly cared, the way lovers or parents or a grandmother were supposed to, by putting her needs first.

The ocean floor grew brighter as one of her stones lit.

"What is it you were thinking, dear?"

"About unconditional love and how I wished it existed for me," she confessed.

Tears filled her mother's eyes as she cupped Payton's cheek. "Oh, you silly girl. You *are* loved unconditionally."

"No—"

"Yes," Mae said, cutting her off. "Yes, Payton, you are. Your father and I didn't leave because of anything you'd done. Were you a trying teenager? Of course. But your fire made you more lovable, not less." She brushed back a lock of Payton's hair from her eyes. "I adore both of my daughters equally. So does your father. We left for your safety. Your father is hunted for what he is, and he didn't want to bring those enemies to your door."

"We needed you!" she cried raggedly. "We needed guidance."

"I was weak. You and Elara are so much stronger than I'll ever be. Able to walk away from what doesn't serve you. Me? No. Rupert owns me, heart and soul."

"No one should own anyone, Mother," she stressed. But her gaze drifted to Dailey, where he entered the ocean.

"Not in the literal sense, no. But I gave my love to him decades ago, and he's treasured it."

"But not the daughters you gave him."

"Payton—"

"Can you please leave me alone?" she begged. "Just until I have more time to come to terms with all of this."

"You should know about your other half."

"Elara has told me enough to survive it." Payton squeezed Mae's hand. "I'm not rejecting you. It's too much while I'm dealing with the fallout of the boots."

"Did you ever consider now, more than ever, you will need to address your emotions? If I'm not mistaken, they are part of the Trickster's lesson plan."

Shit! Her mother was right! Once again, Payton had wanted to avoid the conflict and tuck away the old hurts. Yet, her insecurity was the biggest problem, making her the target of everyone's desire.

"Okay, let's deal with this before Dailey conjures an asteroid to take us out in his frustration."

Mae looked disconcerted, casting him a wary glance. "Is it a real possibility?"

"Yes," Payton said succinctly. Perhaps she was going for shock value, but her mother should be aware not everything was fun and games. The world didn't bend to Rupert and Mae Hawthorne's whims.

"Oh, my."

"You said you were weak, that Father owns you, heart and soul, and you feel Elara and I were able to survive on our own. But what mother does that? What mom and dad jet off, leaving two teenage daughters on their own with no parental guidance?"

"A terrible pair," Mae admitted with a catch in her voice. "But it wasn't your fault, Payton. We love you as much as two selfish parents are capable."

"You freely admit to being self-centered twats?" she asked incredulously.

"Yes." Tears brimmed in Mae's tragic blue eyes, spilling over to trail down her pale cheeks. "Yes, I freely admit it if it means you can find peace with yourself and know you were always cherished, always wanted."

"I'm not, though, am I?" Payton cried. "You, Father, Flo, Dailey… No one could see the real me. Not even Elara did until recently."

"How many times do I have to tell you before you will listen? None of it was your fault." Mae sandwiched Payton's face between her palms. "Hear me, darling girl. Rupert and I were selfish. We couldn't see the real you because we didn't seek to know you. If we did, losing you and your sister would've been impossible to bear. We had to keep an emotional distance for our own sakes, knowing one day we'd be forced to leave you to your own devices."

"And Flo?" Payton's throat ached from suppressed sobs. "Why couldn't my own grandmother give a shit?"

"She did. She gave you and Elara jobs, trying to show you the value of making your way in the world. But at the same time, she set up trust funds, allowing you the freedom to run from your own wedding, remember?"

"We thought those were from you and Dad."

"Oh, we created one for both of you, but those were a contingency, only should you need them."

Again, anger exploded in Payton's chest. "We *did* need them! Elara and I struggled to pay our damned rent."

"No. That's not right. Your apartment was paid for. … oh." Rage clouded Mae's visage, and the waves around them grew forceful. "Mary-Alice Cobb. That… that… *bitch!* Just wait until I get my hands on her!"

Roughly twenty-five yards away, the water grew choppy, churning from a source below the surface. It gained speed as it circled, creating a deadly whirlpool.

"Uh, Mother. If that's you, I'd suggest pulling back your anger." She pointed. "Otherwise, we might drown."

"We can't drown. We're water nymphs." Mae blew out a breath and unclenched her fists. "Your fiancé, however, might."

"*Ex-fiancé.*" And Goddess, didn't it still sting to have lost the dream of forever with him? "What did the wicked old witch do?"

"The apartment was leased through her husband's holding company and paid for through the Hawthorne trust for as long as you girls cared to live there."

"But, we didn't live in Witchmere back then," Payton said.

"No, Harvey Cobb has properties all up and down the coast. Rupert watched to see where the two of you ended up and made sure you found places in the best areas of town."

"We always thought it was dumb luck."

Mae smiled.

"Okay, so back to Mary-Alice… Once we arrived in

Witchmere, she knew us as your daughters. And because we were charged an exorbitant amount for rent, we were swindled," Payton concluded grimly. "Why am I not surprised?"

"I can't believe she'd hate me so much she'd do such an evil thing to you and your sister." Mae was clearly dismayed by the events of the past, but her deeper emotion soothed Payton's residual anger. Knowing her parents hadn't left them to struggle made the world of difference, despite their absence.

"We'll get to the bottom of it," she promised. "In the meantime, how about you tell me how long I need to soak before I'm able to resume my day?"

"Not long." Her mother cocked her blonde head and studied her through thoughtful eyes. "Your energy is lighter. What did I say?"

"You provided for us. All this time, we believed you left us stranded. It's nice to know you didn't."

Her flippers lit again, flaring brightly as if to say, "One issue resolved, a hundred more to go."

CHAPTER NINETEEN

The instant Mae Hawthorne constructed a wall between Payton and him, Dailey experienced an acute withdrawal. Not dissimilar to an addict going without a fix. But the barrier helped calm his arousal, and the cool ocean did the rest. Still, the need to speak to Payton, to hold her and soothe her worries, was strong.

Lying on his back, he floated and stared up at the sun. This was the first peaceful moment he'd had since the morning after her arrest.

As a warlock, he possessed the ability to harness all the elements with ease, but he'd always felt an affinity with water. Whenever he was feeling his lowest after Payton left him, he'd dive into the lake behind his cabin and swim until he was exhausted. The icy plunge numbed not only his body but his mind as well.

He was a broken man in those early days. Hell, he'd remained broken. Perhaps it was why, when the sisters accidentally cursed him, he'd felt such fury. With so few parts of him remaining, they'd removed a vital piece. The only one keeping him human.

They weren't to know that, of course. He'd only come to realize it himself once his emotions returned. And he owed them one hell of an apology for his appalling behavior, for both before and after. Floating here now, recalling the scene in the alley, how petty he'd been, how unforgiving, he could acknowledge deserving everything he'd gotten.

Dailey's love for Payton had been too much for one man to bear, and he hadn't told her how essential she was to his well-being. How she'd filled a hole his father had opened when he'd abandoned them. She believed she wasn't good enough, but all along, he'd believed it about himself, too. She'd proved it by running away and leaving him to face his mother's "I told you so."

And wasn't that the most galling of all? The constant barrage of complaints regarding the woman he'd chosen, what a poor judge of character he was, and nagging about how, if he'd listened to his mother, who always knew best, he'd have saved himself the heartache. Mary-Alice's constant hammering had worn him down, making him ugly inside. He'd been bitter to the point of being nasty to Payton when she first returned.

Instead of pulling her aside and telling her he understood, Dailey had been distant. He'd confirmed for her that she wasn't wanted by anyone, and cemented the point that she'd made the right decision to flee. But in truth, she was better than him by miles. Although she was sassy and quick with a quip, she was never mean. Her sense of fair play was astounding, as was her ability to forgive.

He didn't deserve her.

And he needed to let her go. At least until he got his shit sorted and he could be the man she deserved.

When he did free her, it had to be in a way she would understand *he* was the problem. Not her. Never her.

The fault with his plan? He still loved her. Likely always would. But it didn't mean they should be together. The solution came to him suddenly, causing him to jerk and sink. Dailey broke the surface with a gasp and a plan.

Three lights flared to life, and one remained pulsing while the others snuffed out almost immediately.

"I wonder what those could mean," Mae said with an air of distraction.

Payton glanced over in time to see Dailey go under and come up for a gasping breath. Their eyes locked across the distance, and in his, she would swear she saw regret along with a finality of sorts. Her heart began to hammer in her ears, and she couldn't make out what her mother was saying.

Dailey was going to do something stupid!

She felt it as sure as the shifting sand of the ocean floor beneath her. The desire to tear down the wall, to throw herself into his arms and beg him to reconsider whatever harebrained idea he was forming, paralyzed her. All she could do was stare, as he did, unblinking. Somehow, it had boiled down to this silent communication. A knowing that things would never be the same after this moment.

The stones on her flippers went berserk, creating an underwater light show.

"I'm sorry, Pay," he shouted. "I promise I'll call you soon."

Then he was gone. And with him, all her foolish dreams of reconciliation. But what had she expected? He couldn't find it in himself to forgive her for the way she took off, and neither could she. Her actions had been incredibly foolish; there was no denying it.

"Come to California with me, darling," her mother urged gently.

Could she see the devastation on Payton's face? Did it resemble the same one she'd worn when Mae and Rupert had said their final goodbyes years ago?

"Please leave me alone." Her voice was low and raspy, revealing the anguish she wished to hide. While the young girl inside wanted nothing more than for her mother to hug her and never let go, the adult she'd become wanted the solitude to lick her wounds in private.

"Payton—"

"Just go. Please. It's not a rejection of you, Mother. I just need to be by myself for a bit, okay?"

Concern etched itself in Mae's flawless skin, but she nodded, perhaps recognizing Payton needed to process the grief on her own.

"If you've need of me, call out. But stay close to our elemental source. It will act as a conduit, and you'll require it to survive the transition."

Maybe she didn't want to survive. Maybe she was tired of being a survivor of hardship and abandonment. But she didn't dare say it aloud for fear Mae would stay. So instead, she nodded and suffered through a long hug.

Exiting the water, she sat on the shore. Her flippers converted to flip-flops, exposing her toes. The waves rolled in with their white caps, kissed her feet, then flowed out.

The movement was hypnotic and mind-numbing, allowing her to shut down her feelings.

It wasn't long before she felt the other presence, and she closed her eyes against the intrusion.

"I didn't take ya for a coward, gel."

"Go away, Flo."

Contrary witch that she was, her grandmother sat beside her, kicked off her Birkenstocks, and stretched out her pale, skinny legs.

"I want to be alone."

"I won't say a thing. But I'm not leaving you defenseless. Not again."

Her words were the ones Payton didn't know she needed. A pain built in her chest, tore out through her throat, and bent her double. The warmth of her grandmother's arm around her shoulders was more welcome than anticipated, and she twisted into the embrace to release years of pent-up emotions.

It could've been minutes or hours. Payton couldn't say. Spent, she lay on her side, with her head in Flo's lap. Gentle fingers stroked her hair back from her temple and neck.

"He left me," she said, barely above a whisper. "For good, Flo. I saw it in his face."

"He won't stay gone, child. You are the moth to that boy's flame. From the moment you set foot in Witchmere, his heart was no longer his own."

"But it doesn't mean he wants the trouble I bring."

"Dailey Cobb loves your brand of mischief. You're able to bring a real smile to his face, not the polite kind he gives to the rest of the world. And the spark in his eyes isn't just lust.

It's adoration. Everyone but you can see it. Why do you think Mary-Alice resents you so much?"

"She's a snob, and always said it was because we're from the wrong side of the tracks," Payton argued.

"She knows who your parents are. Knows they come from money. Hell, I set up trusts for you gels as teens, and those accounts rival her children's inheritance any day of the week." Flo tapped her nose. "No, she hates you because you threaten her control over him."

"But he always gives in to her demands, Gran."

The fingers stroking her hair paused, and their faint tremble caused Payton to look up at her.

"That's the first time you've called me Gran," Flo said in an odd voice.

"I'm sorry I was such a shit to you. Thank you for the fake inheritance from our non-existent aunt. It supplemented those cheap-ass bookstore paychecks." They both knew good and well that she and Elara had been grossly underpaid for the area and work they did. But she hadn't been aware of the trust funds before. Her footwear pulsed once, then glowed with a soft light. They both smiled. "Looks like you were one of the people the Trickster's shoes thought deserved a heartfelt apology."

"And I owe you one. I should've worked out visitation with your mother and father before they disappeared. Done more to connect with you when you were teens."

"You couldn't have known where we were," Payton said, pointing out the flaw in logic.

"I found you right after your parents abandoned you," Flo confessed. "I wanted you to stay with me, but I'd failed so miserably with Mae. I guess I figured you were better off without my subpar parenting skills." Her shame hurt Payton on a deeper level. Seemed they both had past failures in common.

"You didn't fail with Mother. She was too obsessed with my father to heed anyone's advice. Honestly, she'd have resented you for getting in her way."

"Part of me understands that," Flo replied through tight lips. "You were never truly alone, gel. I watched over you from afar, especially when you were out on dates, and I chased away anyone who didn't have your best interests at heart. I'll also admit to an influencing spell to bring you here." Payton tensed, and her grandmother was quick to add, "Not to keep you. It was a simple enchantment to encourage you to visit the place, so you could fall in love with it on your own. And you did."

"I fell in love with Witchmere's sheriff, Gran. There's a difference," Payton replied dryly.

"I'll take it."

And because she bothered to actually look without bias, she saw the affection in Flo's expression. "I'll probably leave town again after all this is over, but do you think we can still have a relationship?"

Flo's eyes grew misty. "I'd like nothing better, gel." She cleared her throat. "But instead of leaving, maybe we can find a reason for you to stay. So what are we going to do about that twat Mary-Alice so we can reconnect you and Dailey?"

Payton barked a laugh. She hadn't expected her grandmother as a co-conspirator, but she'd take all the help she could get.

"I'd stay for Dailey. In fact, my only reason for leaving

was because remaining close, without being with him, is more than I can bear."

"Heartache is a bitch." She helped Payton to sit up, then climbed to her feet and held out a hand. "If you're done here, let's go get your man."

Although she allowed Flo to pull her up, Payton shook her head. "I can't set foot in Witchmere. Hermes's magic backfired, and everyone 'wants' me now."

Flo scowled. "That mischievous troll!"

"So I'll stay here until I can figure out what to do, Gran. But thank you for—what the hell?"

Beyond her grandmother's shoulder, twenty men and women were striding from the sea in their birthday suits.

Flo spun to see what had shocked her and swore. "Seems it's not only Witchmere residents who are answering your siren's call, gel. Will you get a load of the size of his—oh!"

Payton wasn't hanging around to see what the Merpeople wanted. Based on the mammoth erection of their leader, she already knew. Gripping her grandmother's hand, she closed her eyes and visualized the attic of the *Never Too Many* bookstore.

CHAPTER TWENTY

"Harry, we have to work fast," Dailey said, the instant he stepped into his brother's office. "Did you or Sloane come up with an antidote to break Mother's spell?"

"No, but Flo and Brelenia may have."

"Tripp's mother was here?"

"She showed up after you left earlier."

He shook his head slowly, trying to wrap his mind around a goddess he didn't know showing up on his behalf. "Why?"

"She was in league with Hermes. Apparently, her husband felt bad and wanted to make sure she didn't leave you to fend for yourself." Harrison walked to the sideboard and poured a drink for both of them. Returning, he handed off a whiskey. "You're going to need this."

"I hate the sound of that."

"Yeah, so did I when Rand and Brelenia showed up on my doorstep."

Harrison's smile didn't reach his eyes, making Dailey worry about what went down.

"You said 'may have.' What's the risk, Harry?"

"You're quick. I'll give you that." After finishing off his drink, his brother crossed to the bookshelf and revealed his ceremony room. "Come on. This needs privacy."

Once they were safely tucked away from prying eyes, Harrison said, "From what Brelenia could tell, it appears whatever has attached itself to Mother is singularly focused on our family. Whether good or bad, she couldn't quite determine which."

Rage bubbled up, trying to cloud Dailey's mind, but he shoved it back down, knowing what would happen if he lost control again.

"How do we break it? The amulets?"

"No, but we can use those for protection after the fact." Harrison flipped open his grimoire and tapped a page. "We unravel it in stages."

"Why not cut it off and be done?"

"If we rush it, the backlash could snap your tether back in place."

"Tether?" Dailey's stomach churned. His brother made it sound like he'd been leashed like a savage junkyard dog.

"I'm sorry, D."

His brother's eyes held sympathy for Dailey's cause.

"It's not your fault, Harry." Running an impatient hand through his hair, he said, "Tell me about this process."

"As I said, it has to happen in stages. The quickest we can manage will be three days."

The way he abandoned Payton on the beach rose up in

his mind, and Dailey felt sick again. She'd seen his intent, recognized it. But if he didn't become his own man, free of outside influence, he would never be the person she deserved. He'd hoped it was a simple matter of countering his mother's handiwork, but it wasn't.

"I don't have that kind of time."

"Any sooner, and it could fail, D. Most likely it will."

"Fuck!" He was feeling savage, wanting to tear the heads off teddy bears and kick over lemonade stands. "There will be withdrawal. There always is," he said grimly. "Tell me what you know."

"Headaches and anger on day one, as clarity hits."

"Sounds about right. Day two?"

"Emotional spikes as memories and feelings align properly."

Dailey grimaced. "And finally?"

"Hopefully, you're free of her. But we'll need to have a failsafe in place in case it doesn't work."

"How long will it take to make what we need and perform the ceremony?"

Harrison shrugged. "An hour. Two at the most."

"Can you do that while I write Payton a letter?"

His brother frowned.

"I have to say goodbye, Harry. In case this goes sideways. Cobb power is at the root of Witchmere, and she draws her strength here." Indeed, the Cobbs were the founders of Witchmere, and because of her family heritage, Mary-Alice Cobb had refused to take her husband's name, insisting he take hers. "It will take a Christmas miracle if this goes well."

Sloane entered on his last comment. "Witchmere has

never been shy of those, D. We have our own Make-A-Dream-Happen crew."

He snorted. "For tourists, not for the residents."

She gave a careless shrug, reminding him of Payton with that action.

"You and Harry collect what we need and prep the room. I'll only be fifteen minutes."

Leaving them, Dailey used Harrison's desk to pour out his heart, what was left of it, on paper. When he was done, he checked his watch. Five minutes was plenty of time to find Archer and return.

He arrived at the cabin to find the gargoyle clan gathered outside.

"Why aren't you inside where it's warm?" he asked.

Cecil pointed skyward. "We don't trust them. If they have us all in one building..."

"Ah." No words would reassure them that the dragons wouldn't torch the house, so Dailey remained quiet on the subject. "Roche, can I see you for a minute?"

They walked a short distance away, and he held out the envelope. "Will you give this to Payton? She'll return here soon. I can feel it. And when she does, tell her I'm sorry."

"You should deliver it yourself, Cobb."

"I can't. I'm not able to get close without..." Heat crept up his neck. "I'm not able to get close."

"Will she bring down the world when she reads this?" Archer asked, eyeing the letter with a frown.

"I don't think so. She's not the one with a meteor problem," he replied with a wry, self-mocking smile.

"Call it instinct, but I don't feel right about this."

"I wouldn't ask if it weren't important, Archer," he said, appealing to the man's softer side.

With a nod, the protector tucked it into his coat pocket. "My people will need to rest in a few hours. Twelve on, twelve off, remember?"

"Yes. I'm going to send Harry and Sloane to create a ward when I'm done there."

"Done? What are you planning?"

"Nothing to bring the town to its knees. Stay calm," Dailey advised.

Archer narrowed his all-seeing eyes. "But something."

"I intend to sever my mother's hold over me. She put it in place long ago."

"I suspected as much," the protector said grimly.

He appeared uncomfortable, prompting Dailey's suspicions.

Trying to keep the dawning horror from his voice, he asked, "Did my family bind you to this place?"

The answer was in Archer's direct stare.

"Christ!" The hits kept coming! "The only thing strong enough to hold you would be blood magic, Roche. Is that what they used? Do you know?"

"It was a long time ago, and I've made peace with it."

"No. No, no, no." Dailey released a string of savage curses. "I'm going to reverse this. Count on it."

"You can't."

"Why?" he demanded.

"It will kill my line. The first Cobb made it foolproof."

"We have gods and Titans, Roche. Surely they are stronger than an ancient warlock who's been dead for half a century."

"Go do what you must to break your mother's spell, Dailey. We'll discuss this after your drama's done. I promise."

Feeling oddly sentimental, he hugged the bear of a man. Archer Roche was the only guy who made him feel both small and yet as if his opinion mattered. "Thank you for your service to Witchmere and for helping Payton. I owe you, and I'll do whatever I can to free you."

With a nod, the gargoyle laird strode away.

Closing his eyes, Dailey visualized his brother's office, returning in time to find his mother snooping about.

"What are you doing here?" he asked coldly.

She turned with a gasp. "Dailey!"

Her guilt stained her cheeks for a brief instant before she pasted on her standard arrogance.

"I asked you a question, Mother."

Smiling, she approached and reached out, but he snapped his fingers, encasing himself in a protective shield he used when confronting the shadier characters in town. With a vampire-like hiss, she drew back, sensing before touching that she'd receive a nasty shock.

"What are you doing?" she asked with an offended look.

"I think you know."

"It's that girl again, isn't it? She's gotten into your head." Expression ugly, she balled her fists. "When are you going to learn, Dailey? She's no good!"

A green mist rose from the skin of her exposed hands, drifting toward him. When it encountered his shield, it split and slithered along either side, seeking an opening.

"Mother!" Sloane's reprimand was the single snapped word.

The smoke evaporated as if it never existed, and Mary-Alice Cobb looked like she'd taken a hammer to the head. Her surprise was too convincing, leaving Dailey wondering whether her influence was intentional or the unintended result of her desperate need to control.

"Mother," he said softly, catching her attention. "Did you see the mist?"

"Mist? What mist?" She frowned as if he'd lost his mind. Either she was the best actor he'd ever seen, or she wasn't aware it existed. "Stop playing games, Dailey. What is going on, and why did you use a repellent against me?"

"It is a shield against evil, Mother," he replied slowly, watching her closely for signs of artifice. There were none, and he was forced to reevaluate her part in his control. If not her, then who? And had that witch or warlock purposefully used her as a tool?

"I'm not evil! How dare you!"

Across the distance, he met Sloane's bemused stare. She'd seen it, too, and her confusion was great.

"Mother, I think you should sit down. We have a story to tell you, and you're at the heart of it."

Harrison entered through the hallway door, as their sister had, and Dailey could only assume there was a secret passage, allowing him to protect the ceremony room from discovery in situations like this.

"Careful, Dailey," he warned.

Thinking back on their entire lives, he couldn't recall witnessing her do anything truly horrendous. Yes, she was controlling, but was she any different from any other helicopter parent? When she believed no one was looking, she slipped strays food, then doubled down on her efforts to ensure they found a home. Many times, she'd visited residents, ensuring they had enough food in tight times. She'd secretly met with their employers to press them into giving bonuses and raises.

Surely she wasn't all bad, right? Or was it the enchantment swaying him to see what she wanted him to? How was he to know for certain?

"Mother, I know you put a spell on me. I want you to voluntarily remove it."

"Dailey James Cobb! What in the Goddess's name are you talking about? This had better not be another one of that Hawthorne girl's flights of fancy."

He shared a glance with his siblings. Both appeared as confused as he was, and it served to make him feel better.

Harrison approached and squatted in front of her. "Mom. We know there's a spell on him. Others have smelled it. Tripp deflected it earlier today when you tried to control Dailey. If you know anything about this, you need to come clean."

Her horror wasn't feigned as she shifted her gaze from Harrison to him. Relief made Dailey's knees feel like jelly.

"She didn't know, Harry," he said. "She didn't know."

"How could she not?" Sloane argued. "Tripp deflected it."

"I don't have an answer. But I deal with people every day and wade through their lies. I can promise you, she's telling the truth."

"Of course, I am!" Mary-Alice's indignation was in fine form. "When have I ever lied to you children? Never! You may not wish to hear the unvarnished truth, but I give it to you anyway. How else are you to make the appropriate decisions in life?" As she warmed to her rant, the green mist rose from her skin.

"Fuck!" Dailey raised a hand, encapsulating his mother in a bubble. "It's built into her self-righteousness. She's not aware of influencing others."

CHAPTER TWENTY-ONE

"You can't stay here," Flo said once they'd landed. "Others will answer the call as soon as they sense your presence."

Payton hurried to the window to peer out. Sure enough, people were stopping in their tracks and lifting their heads like hounds scenting a rabbit. The few she knew to be wolf shifters registered her magical pheromones first, and she met the conflicted eyes of Rowan's brother, Bohdan. Although crazy about another woman, he would find it difficult to fight the allure.

"Yeah, I gotta go." She kissed Flo's cheek. "I'll call you as soon as I get to Dailey's cabin."

"I'll go, too. There's still a little witchcraft left in these old bones. No one will touch my gels."

"Are you sure? What about the shop?" Payton asked.

"Rowan's watching it for me."

Having her friend downstairs was actually helpful.

Bohdan wouldn't make it farther than his sister. She'd kick his ass if he tried to get to Payton.

She had a moment's pause as she considered Rowan's behavior in the bar. Yeah, there was no way she'd be safe in this attic for long.

"Okay, Gran, let's go."

Their next stop was the clearing in front of the cabin, where they discovered Archer Roche waiting for them.

"Dailey figured you'd make your way back here," he said by way of greeting. "He said to give you this."

Payton stared at the letter in his hand, fearing what it contained. Odds were it was a standard Dear Jane letter, and the old "it's not you, it's me."

Flo, tuned into her inner turmoil, accepted the envelope on her behalf.

"Where is the bloody coward?" she growled.

Archer's mouth tipped up at the corners, but he shook his head. "Don't know, ma'am."

"It's okay, Gran." Payton managed a smile she didn't feel and grabbed the letter from her hand. "Thanks, Archer. Is anyone in the cabin?"

"Elara. Greer and Cecil are outside at the back corners, keeping watch." His countenance took on a forbidding expression. "Those blasted dragons are patrolling from the air, ensuring no one gets close."

"You make it seem like a bad thing," she replied dryly, understanding all too well the bad blood between the two. "At least they are doing something noble, right?"

"Likely, they've agreed so they can set the townsfolk on fire if they venture too close. They're a bloodthirsty lot."

Stretching up, Payton kissed his cheek. "Thank you for setting aside your distrust to protect me."

His rough-hewn expression softened. "It's my pleasure, Miss."

"It's Payton. No need to be formal among friends."

Although he smiled, he didn't reply.

"But I can't hide out here forever," she said. "These cursed shoes are going to require a sacrifice, and I don't want it to be any of you. If we can put our heads together and figure this out, that would be great."

"Elara and Tripp were prepared to jump into the volcano for each other. Not that I'm suggesting you do that," he said quickly, when she gasped in dismay. "I'm merely saying, you and Dailey, if you're meant to be, should find a working solution together, rather than apart."

She held up the envelope. "Why do I think that's easier said than done?"

"If you want my opinion, he's a fool for not staying to work through your problems."

The kindness in Archer's hazel eyes didn't soothe the ache left by Dailey's vanishing act, but she appreciated it all the same.

"I left him first. He didn't deserve the fallout."

"We all know the reason, and so does he." He shook his ginger-haired head. "I wouldn't want Mary-Alice for a mother-in-law. Not many would."

"Thank you."

Payton and Flo headed for the cabin. When they got to the porch, she said, "You go in and conjure dinner with Elara. I'll join you shortly." She waved the letter. "I should see what he has to say."

"Let me know if I need to hunt him down and skin him alive."

"Extreme, but I may take you up on it."

After giving her a tight hug, her grandmother left her alone.

Payton sat on the glider, tucked her legs under her, and ran a nail under the flap. Letter in hand, she channeled her courage and unfolded the paper.

"This is bad, D."

"I know, Harry."

Their mother had worked herself up to a frenzy. And the crazier she became, the more mist seeped from her skin.

"She can't remain as mayor," Sloane said in a low voice. "Not if whatever is inside of her comes out to play when she's thwarted."

"I know that, too. But how the hell do we separate it from her and her from the job?"

"Brelenia might have a suggestion," Harrison said, with a clinical eye on their mother, who sat across the room fuming. The green mist had enveloped the entire interior of her bubble, yet she seemed unaware of its existence. "And I agree. I don't believe this is her own doing."

"It begs the question, who *is* doing it?" Sloane replied, appearing ill at ease. "I hate to think I've misjudged her all these years."

"You haven't, Sloane." Harrison wrapped an arm around her shoulders like he had when they were kids. His protective instincts for their sister had always been strong. Perhaps he'd subconsciously recognized her need to feel loved, since their mother had been so stingy about giving in to those warmer emotions, especially where her daughter was concerned. "She's still an overbearing mother. She's just one with a built-in toxic gas."

Despite the seriousness of the situation, Dailey snorted a laugh. A cartoon image of their mother releasing toxic gas floated about in his mind, and he had the urge to pick up a pencil to sketch it. Once, when he was a kid, he would've. But his mother had taken away his pencils and lectured him, saying Cobbs held worthwhile jobs, not those of artists, actors, or non-societal contributors. A part of his younger self's soul had died the day she took his sketchbook away, and he'd refused to participate in museum field trips. Instead, he'd stayed home and studied for some exam or another, under the proud eye of his mother.

"How do we get ahold of Brelenia?" he asked, feeling a sudden melancholy. "Maybe she's encountered a situation like ours before. I still don't understand why she'd failed to mention this part earlier. Did she not pick up on it?"

"Rand left his number. I'll give him a ring," Harrison replied.

It didn't take long before they had their answer.

"A triad?" Sloane asked. "Who here in town would constitute one?"

"The Hawthornes," Harrison said with a concerned glance at Dailey. "Elara, Payton, and Flo might count as one."

"No." Dailey would never believe it. Flo bore no love for Mary-Alice, and neither did Payton, but there was no way the Hawthorne women were involved. Not even accidentally. They were inherently good. "It would need to go back decades, Harry. Elara and Payton didn't know what they were until last year."

"There are three Sandersons, but again, age is a factor," Sloane said. "Who would've been around longer than us?"

"Only the Camdens have been around as long as the Cobbs," their mother said from her seat. She sent Sloane an unfathomable glance.

"Bradford is a douche canoe, Mother, no doubt, but he—"

"His father is one of three," Dailey said slowly as the truth dawned. "Bradford the Second, Orson, and Archibald. But why target you?" he asked her.

"Orson loved me," she said simply. "But I left him for your father, Harvey. The minute he strolled into town, I knew I was meant to be with him." Her mouth tightened in pain. "The Camdens were known as The Unholy Triad. What they wanted, they got."

"And you married me off to one of them," Sloane stated flatly. "And Mother of the Year award goes to… Mary-Alice Cobb."

"I…" More green smoke filled the bubble.

"We'll discuss it when you're free of whatever has hold of you," Harrison said. "Right now, we have to find a way to ensure they can no longer influence her, if they are."

"Does this mean my breaking away just got harder?" Dailey asked.

"No. I suspect it's easier." His brother nodded, as if he'd reached a conclusion. "Wait here, D."

The room was eerily silent while he was gone, but what did they really have to talk about? Sloane was stewing over their mother pushing her to marry a man she didn't love,

Dailey was questioning his entire existence, and Mary-Alice was bizarrely quiet for once in her life.

Harrison returned and handed both Sloane and him a vial, keeping a third for himself. "The antidote, tweaked to exclude Camden influence from our lives. Bottoms up, gang."

"What about Mother?" It didn't sit well with Dailey to leave her infected by the Triad.

"That's going to need a spell with surgical precision. One we haven't built yet." He cocked his head. "Are you okay locking her up for a while, Dailey?"

"I don't love it. But I'd rather contain a known risk than pretend everything is fine. She can't be left free in this state."

"What about the secret room?" Sloane asked in a low voice. "It was meant to keep her out, but with a little magical engineering, would it keep her in and the Triad's spell out?"

Dailey considered her suggestion from every angle. "I'll defer to you, but I think she might be better in the holding cell in the station's basement. The one I reserve for our kind."

"I can't disagree," Harrison said, nodding.

Surprisingly, Sloane was the one to object. "I don't care how she feels about me, fellas. But don't destroy what's left of your relationships with her. If you can remove whatever that *thing* is, you may have something salvageable left over." She cast an unreadable glance at their mother. "She won't forgive you if you humiliate her in front of the town by hauling her to jail."

Dammit, Sloane was right!

"Let's drink this, see what sort of clarity it brings, and decide after," Dailey suggested.

They nodded their agreement, and as one, they removed the caps to down the potion.

His body's reaction was immediate. As Harrison indicated, a headache and dizziness followed. He could almost feel the taut wire connecting him to his mother. Disregarding his brother's earlier caution, Dailey pictured an axe and severed the cord.

Mary-Alice cried out, and had he possessed use of his limbs or even a clear mind, he'd have gone to her. But fortunately for him, he remained where he was, because he wouldn't have fared well close to her.

The protective shield encasing her stretched and strained under the force of the mist's need to reach them.

Behind Dailey, the door to the hallway opened, and he turned to find the Trickster.

"Cobb, we have a problem brewing at your place," Hermes said.

Then he heard the echo of Payton's enraged scream, accompanied by a howling wind.

"What the fuck was that?" Dailey asked, shaken. "Is she hurt?"

"You might be the best person to answer that," Hermes replied. "Get there."

CHAPTER TWENTY-TWO

Wildfire,

From the first moment I set eyes on you, I lost my ability to think straight and the will to care that I had. Throughout our relationship, loving you has never been the hard part. I've done it easily, fiercely, without pause. Those emotions come naturally when it comes to you.

Being worthy of it does not.

You believe you're the one who isn't enough, Pay, but I promise you, I've never met anyone as pure-hearted and open. You give of yourself without agenda. It's only right for you to expect the same in return.

Only I can't give it.

I've spent years letting other people steer my choices, remaining silent when I should've spoken up. I told myself it was my sense of duty. Loyalty to the mother who sacrificed everything for her children. Yet the truth is simpler.

It was pure fear.

Fear of standing alone. Of disappointing the woman who raised me. Of becoming the man my father was when he walked away. So I stayed and took every bit of the shit she handed out.

Every single time I chose the easier path, you paid the price. I can see that now. See how you felt small while carrying more than your share. My expectations, left unchecked and unexamined, became another weight on your shoulders. Then, I foolishly punished you for leaving instead of asking why you had run in the first place. Our home should've been your shelter from a world that treated you poorly. It wasn't, and I'm entirely to blame.

You deserve a partner who chooses you openly. Every day. Without apology. Without hesitation.

Under my mother's spell, I was never him. I'm not sure I can ever be until I break her hold. I love you too much to keep asking you to bleed while I sort myself out. You don't deserve to be trapped in a future built on hope alone.

So I am letting you go.

Not because you failed me or because loving you is a mistake. How could it be? You were the truest thing in my life, Payton Hawthorne. I am stepping aside because freedom is the one gift I never afforded you, and it is long overdue.

Live boldly, laugh often, and burn bright enough for both of us, okay?

You were never the problem, my darling Wildfire. You were my miracle. And you will ALWAYS be good enough. Hell, better than good—the best thing to grace another's life.

Forever yours,

Lee

. . .

Her heart spasmed so sharply, aching so badly, she thought she was having heart failure. Drawing her next breath hurt. The paper drifted to the deck boards as she clutched her chest and struggled to inhale. And when the sobs came, it felt like her soul pouring out through her tears.

Dailey, like everyone before him, claimed she wasn't the problem; *he* was. But once again, someone she loved more than life itself had chosen to walk away. Leaving her like yesterday's trash by the side of the road, or in his case, stranded on a beach in Goddess-knew-what country.

In the entire time since meeting him, she'd never seen him as the villain. She hadn't been angry at his choices because she saw his duty for what it was.

Now?

Yeah, now she was fucking pissed!

Thunder rumbled as charcoal storm clouds rolled in. Lightning popped with alarming frequency as she screamed from the depths of her soul.

Behind her, the window panes shattered, and the door slammed back on its hinges as the shingles rippled from the increasing wind speed. Around the property, trees bent, snapping under hurricane-force gusts. The heavens opened, releasing sheets of slashing rain.

"You're a fucking coward, Dailey Cobb!" she hollered, stalking down the steps and into the driveway. "Hear me! *You're a fucking coward!* And I *hate* you!"

The ground shook beneath her feet, and the earth split open, creating a wide-mouthed moat around the cabin.

Her hair, naturally wavy, grew in length, curling tighter, and her skin turned bioluminescent, giving off a soft blue hue of deep-water jellyfish.

"If you ever dare show your stupid face again, I will *smite* you!" she called out, and her threat echoed into the darkening space around her.

The air thickened, crackling with an energy not her own. Her anticipation hung in the air. She prayed he'd heard and was dumb enough to return so she could make good her promise.

But instead of him, her father weathered the raging storm to reach her.

In his eyes resided deep regret, despair, and oddly, pride.

"Payton. My little Sunseed." The wind whipped his thick gray hair, as the rains plastered his clothes to his body. He moved with a grace not known to older men, with no signs of aging or pain. When he reached her, he simply stared, as if he expected her to be happy he'd shown up.

What she truly wanted was for him to sweep her into his embrace as he had when she was small. When she believed love was the most essential thing in the world. Growing up, there had never been any doubt she was a daddy's girl. And right then, she wished she could throw herself in his arms and sob her grief for the worst rejection of all.

But she wouldn't.

She was done giving her power to others so they could carelessly toss it aside.

"What are you doing here?" she asked coldly.

"I came to tell you that you're perfect, and any fault is not your own. To tell you I love you, as I should've done every day of your life."

She scoffed. "Isn't it too little, too late?"

His blue eyes, a mirror of hers, studied her face with undisguised affection. "I don't believe so, no."

"Let me take a stab at why you arrived at this particular moment," she sneered. "Your wild Titan hybrid daughter is losing her shit, ready to tear down the fucking world, and you—hero that you are—have taken it upon yourself to calm her down rather than allow her to risk the Gods' wrath. How am I doing?"

"Partially true, yes." He stepped closer. "I've also come to re-bind your abilities."

His comment was a blow to the solar plexus. She and Elara had only started developing what they should've had all along, but were denied due to their parents' fear of being hunted.

"You would steal my magic? *Again?*" Her disbelief made her hoarse.

"I have no choice, Sunseed. You're about to cause untold damage, and the Gods will send their greatest warriors."

"Let them," she snarled. In her blind fury, she was ready to take everyone on single-handedly.

"You will not be put to death on my watch," he said, his voice laced with steel.

"What does it matter?" she cried. "Tell me, Father, who will really care when I'm gone?"

"What a ridiculous question! I would. Your mother, Florence, and Elara all would. Your friends."

She shook her head for every name mentioned. "Not you. Not mother. You'll hardly notice. As for Elara and my friends, they'll all be better off."

"And Dailey?" Elara asked from behind her.

Payton spun to find her sister, mother, and grandmother at the base of the steps, tears streaming down their faces.

But for the first time in her life, she was unmoved. Cold was creeping in, icing her heart over.

"He can go screw himself for all I care," she said emotionlessly. "He no longer factors into my decisions."

"Even if I said I made a mistake?" he asked from behind her.

To her ears, Dailey sounded regretful, but she didn't give a rat's ass. She was fed up. What had laying her heart on the line, time and time again, ever done for her?

She held out her hands, observing the bluish glow of her skin deepen. She tilted her chin up, closed her eyes, and reveled in nature's full glory as it slapped her skin. Drawing from the electricity dancing along the air's current, she held it within her grasp as she faced him.

"You didn't make a mistake, Dailey Cobb. I did by choosing a *weakling*," she spat right before hurling a bolt in his direction.

From nowhere, Hermes stepped into his path and accepted the brunt of the charge. He screamed his agony, bringing the gargoyles to the yard. An instant later, a dragon circled, blocking out the remaining light.

Payton geared up for a second strike, this time with the intent to obliterate her original target. As she raised her arms, Vorren plunged downward and plucked her from the ground like a hawk snatching a chicken. His talons became her cage as he soared upward with a mighty roar.

CHAPTER TWENTY-THREE

Dailey was, to put it plainly, stunned! All his training as a cop flew out the window as a dragon, the size of two 747s combined, swooped down and stole the woman he loved.

"Stop him!" he shouted at the others. As Titans, Payton's father and sister had more power in their pinky toes than he did in his entire body.

He bent to check Hermes, who was convulsing. A lightning strike was instantaneous, and either a person lived or they didn't. Burns, heart and respiratory problems, neurological issues, seizures… all normal, but Hermes was a god. He should've been able to absorb the bolt. Surely he'd believed it, too, or he wouldn't have jumped in the way, right?

"Don't," Greer warned, stopping Dailey from touching him as Archer and Cecil tended to the Trickster. "Whatever she hit him with wasn't standard electrical lightning." Her eyes were somber when she added, "She fully intended to kill."

Payton wanted him dead.

The reality washed over him, and he sat back on his heels, dropping his head in his hands. He'd been too late to retrieve his goodbye letter.

As if to reinforce his conclusion, the breeze carried the paper to him, blowing it upward with a second gust and covering his face. The ink had smeared, making what he'd written illegible, but he knew it by heart. He found no reason for her fury, other than his decision to set her free.

And then it clicked.

Everyone left her, and his perceived defection was the final straw.

"Oh my god," he whispered achingly. "What the hell did I do?"

"You sent her over the edge to madness," Florence said scathingly. "You're as thoughtless and twisted as your damned mother is."

"I thought I'd make it back in time to stop Archer from giving it to her," he said lamely. But his actions were inexcusable. He'd broken her heart, crushing her in the worst way possible. "I have to fix this."

"You've done enough, young man," Rupert snapped. "When I find my daughter and bring her home, you'd better have vacated the area. Because I won't stop her from killing you."

"Dad, stop!" Elara shut her eyes as if concentrating, and when she opened them, the world around them had returned to its standard setting.

The blue sky overhead was an affront to the churning

emotions inside him. Dailey was left wondering if Payton's similar emotions were why she had called down nature's fury, and with it the torrential downpour.

Elara placed a hand on his shoulder. "It's not your fault, Dailey. It's been a lifetime of rejection for her."

She approached Archer and Cecil. "Back off, fellas. Let me see if I can remove what she attached to him."

"No, Elara. Not alone," her father warned. "Whatever she struck him with wasn't only Titan magic. She was harnessing Trickster and water nymph power, too."

As father and daughter worked, it occurred to Dailey that it could be him lying there, had Hermes not reacted as quickly as he had. Would anyone have bothered to try to save *him*? Doubtful. But what really rubbed salt in the wound was how intent Payton had been to cause his suffering.

Striding into the cabin, he got down what he needed to scry for her: a map of the world, a smoky quartz crystal, candles, and salt for a protective circle. Next, he cleared the table and set out his supplies.

He was going to find her, and when he did, they were going to have a heart-to-heart. No misunderstandings, just the Goddess's honest truth. And if she still wanted him dead after, well, she'd be doing him a favor. Without her, he was dead inside anyway.

Striding into the bedroom, he withdrew a locket she'd forgotten in her rush to leave him the first time. It had meant something to her once, and he was surprised she never asked him for it back. Opening it, he studied the images of them: one from their first date and the other from right after their engagement. It hurt like fucking hell to look at those pictures, and he'd avoided doing it until now.

Goddess! They were so happy then.

Determined they would be again, Dailey placed the necklace on the table and dangled the crystal above the map.

"By will and love, by pull unseen,
All paths we crossed and ties between,
Bring this man to where you stand,
Lead me true, obey my command."

The pendant spun in tight circles, landing on nothing. The movement was concerning in itself, but not immediately finding a location was terrifying. He'd always been able to scry with success. Was the dragon's power cloaking her?

Whipping out his phone, he dialed Tripp.

"Nightshade."

"It's Dailey."

"Yeah, that's what came up on the caller ID."

"Wiseass." Exhaling a steadying breath, he said, "I can't find Payton. I've tried scrying, but I'm coming up with nothing. I have to admit, man, I'm freaking out."

"Elara said Vorren took her. We've already got Cory tracking them."

He strode to the window.

Tripp was standing beside Hermes and Elara, watching the cabin.

With a frustrated growl, Dailey disconnected and strode outside. "You could've told me you were here."

Although amusement danced in the demigod's dark eyes, he didn't outright grin. "If Vorren took her, it was to save the people here. He's a royal in Drakoryth, Cobb, and it means he's very much aware of the need to keep strong political ties to other countries and realms. She'll be safe, and hopefully, when found, in a better frame of mind."

"I have to find her sooner rather than later. I can't let this misunderstanding remain between us." He felt exposed, but he was tired of hiding behind duty and quips. "I love her, and the letter was the dumbest thing I've done to date."

Elara rubbed his back as she presented him with the newly dried and restored paper. "It's not, Dailey. You believed you were setting her free to live her life. You had no way of knowing she'd react badly."

"But I should've expected it. She's made no secret of how much it hurt when everyone walked away, and there I was, adding to her list of people who didn't stick." He ran his hand through his hair and huffed out a breath in frustration. "I'm so goddamn stupid!"

Hermes glanced skyward, a frown on his face. "No meteors in the last few hours. Have you curbed your earth-destroying anger issues, Badge Boy?"

The observation surprised Dailey. With all the drama, he'd forgotten about his ability to light the planet up if he lost his shit. But thinking back over the day, the change had to have happened at the beach. Floating in the water had given him clarity, and his emotions had snapped back into place.

"Maybe I'm cured. For the moment at least. But I'm reserving the right to knock a few people out with rocks." He glanced at the gargoyles. "No offense."

Greer, bless her, laughed, and amusement danced in

Archer's eyes. Cecil scowled, making them all aware of who lacked the sense of humor in their group.

"Where did your parents go, Elara?" Dailey asked with a quick glance around.

"To their home. They fear the concentration of energy will bring down the Gods on all of us."

Made sense. Between gargoyles, dragons, Titans, a Trickster, a demigod, and the least threatening of all, him—a warlock—there was a helluva lot of firepower in a small amount of space.

Too much.

Was it because of them that Payton was able to gain the abilities she had? Was it just a matter of tapping into the collective?

"Hermes, tell me more about those boots."

"Like what?" The poor guy still appeared disoriented, and with every movement he made, he winced.

Dailey felt for him, but he couldn't waste time being solicitous when he had to find Payton.

"Would they allow the wearer to channel other beings' magic? Or maybe pull from the earth's pool of power?"

The Trickster's dark brows met as he considered the question. Eventually, he nodded. "Previous to Elara, I'd have said no. But with each incarnation, her mastery grew. Their abilities morphed as well. They've consumed a small amount from each owner to take on a life of their own."

"So it's possible they influenced her stunt today? Maybe her more explosive emotions weren't solely her own?"

"No. She was enraged," Elara said. "I felt it before my father showed up."

Daily acknowledged her point with a nod. "But the

energy manipulation, the glowing blue skin, the desire to kill, that doesn't seem normal to me."

"Agreed," Hermes said tiredly. "It was extreme."

"How do we resolve the issue if she won't see reason?" Tripp asked.

Dailey whipped around to stare. "Why won't she be able to see reason?"

"Elara didn't at first." Her fiancé cast her an apologetic glance. "Your emotions ran high."

"It's true, but eventually, I came around. Payton will, too."

Yet Dailey was left to wonder how if she weren't here to listen to his apology.

"What about a blood-to-blood spell?" he asked. "Would it reach across the realms and bring her back, or us to her?"

"It might," Tripp replied, but his expression said, 'No fucking way!' "I'm not comfortable with Elara donating even a drop of hers. It will make her too vulnerable should anyone obtain it."

"What about a burn-after-reading clause?" Greer asked, casting a glance at her fellow clan members. "It's what we used to do ages ago to protect against enemies. It could work for her, right?"

Elara appeared intrigued as she met Dailey's gaze and nodded.

"How would that work?" he asked. He was unwilling to endanger another, but if Elara were game, he'd try anything to get Payton back.

"It's built into the spell and will burn up the blood along with the map used to find her," Archer explained. "But considering she may not be in this realm, it may not work.

And any blood spilled on behalf of finding her will simply roll around aimlessly searching for her without relief."

"So that's out." Dailey shook his head as Elara objected. "No. If Vorren took her to Drakoryth, which appears likely since I couldn't locate her with her necklace, then there's no point." He looked at Tripp. "Will Cory take me to Drakoryth if I ask him?"

"No, but I will," a gravelly voice said.

A sulfurous stench filled the air around, and Dailey almost gagged for the second time today. In his lifetime, he's seen a lot and smelled even worse. It was doubtful he'd grow used to the overpowering odor whenever these dragons dropped their invisibility cloaks.

"Christ alive, that's awful!" Elara cried. "You need to carry air freshener with you if you're going to poison the atmosphere like that!"

The dragon laughed and sidled up to Greer. "And you, woman, do you find my scent offensive?"

"I find your entire species offensive, as well you know," she retorted with her chin raised in challenge.

Nazek surprised Dailey when he chuckled and blew her a kiss. Color climbed her neck, but she didn't look away as he continued to stare. The space between the two was charged, and one could almost see the current if they squinted hard enough.

Abruptly, as if he wasn't just using his archaic brand of flirting on the female, Nazek turned to Dailey, saying, "Are you ready to go, Warlock?"

"Yes."

"You should conjure protection for yourself. Our

kingdom isn't friendly to those such as you, and breathing will sear the lining of your puny human lungs."

"He means a gas mask," Tripp explained, clearing Dailey's confusion. "But that alone won't save you."

The demigod walked the short distance to a nearby tree, broke off a branch, and stripped it. As he strode back, he manipulated the leaves into the shape of a gas mask.

"*Ei vitalem sustentationem praebe,*" he said before cupping his fingers around it, bringing it to his mouth, and blowing.

Provide him with life support.

A necessary enchantment, but still bone-chilling for Dailey to think of himself needing life support.

Tripp presented him with what looked to be a clear, plastic face covering. "It will convert whatever air their world contains into oxygen."

"What about Payton? How can she survive there?"

"She's a Titan, Dailey," Hermes pointed out. "Her body will always adapt to save itself. Just as her nymph's half can breathe underwater."

"Maybe I should go too," Elara suggested, worry in her expression and tone. "If anyone has a chance of stopping her from killing him, it's me."

Dailey handed the protective mask back to Tripp. "Can you charm it to stay on when she tries to rip my face off?"

CHAPTER TWENTY-FOUR

Vorren took Payton to a world unlike anything she'd ever seen before. Where she believed there to be a cluster of snow-capped trees on a cliff, his single, deafening roar opened a portal to the breathtaking kingdom of Drakoryth. And mirroring Earth's realm, the landscape was a winter wonderland, making Payton question whether they had their own version of Old Saint Nick or not.

Were tiny dragon children running around, eyes sparkling with excitement as they anticipated the jolly man showing up with presents? A single glance at the village assured her they weren't celebrating here. There was no tree lit in the center of town. No colorful lights, wreaths, or decorations of any kind. Drakoryth Castle, though filled with ornate artifacts and stunning to view, was also barren of holiday decor.

And didn't it make her sad?

She loved Christmas. From the time she'd been a small

child, her mother had made sure to create an enchanting holiday for them. Trees with the works for every room, with presents under the tallest, resting in a place of honor in front of their living room window. No one passing their home could miss the joyous sight.

She and Elara had gotten out of the habit of celebrating because funds were always tight in their younger years. But Dailey had gifted the holiday happiness back to her in the short time they'd been together.

Dailey.

Goddess, she was exhausted on every front.

"Come, Payton," Vorren said gently. "I shall show you to the guest quarters. A server will bring up a tray."

The bedroom, with its ginormous bath and sitting rooms, was five times that of Elara's apartment. The four-poster bed was as inviting as she'd ever seen.

"Good night, Dragon Daddy. Thanks for the save."

"I had the feeling you might regret murdering your mate." Though he smiled, the concern in his eyes was very real. "Will you be all right, or should I send my sister to you?"

"I'm fine. But if you don't mind, I'd like to be alone now."

"As you wish." He raised her hand and kissed her knuckles, as if the gesture were ingrained. She absently noted that her skin no longer resembled a Smurf's.

"Sleep well, Payton."

The day's events had finally caught up to her, and her fear of the future dimmed as her eyes closed in sleep. It felt as if she'd just dozed off when someone spoke, calling her name.

"Payton," the voice said again.

But she wasn't ready to face reality, and there was comfort in sleep.

She batted away the hand stroking her skin.

"Pay, you have to wake up." The voice was Dailey's, loving and kind, but muffled as if he were underwater. Yet he couldn't be here in Dragon Eye-Candyland. He'd never survive the atmosphere.

Curling into the tempting warmth of the human-sized pillow beside her, she allowed sleep to take her back under.

"Wildfire."

"Dailey," she murmured, snuggling closer to the heat.

"You must get up now. Your skin is too dry, and you need a soak, sweetheart."

She licked her lips, feeling the roughness indicative of soon-to-be cracked skin. Yes, she needed water, or at least a good lip balm. Still, she resisted. He'd only been gone a few hours, and she missed him. An ache took the place of the coldness she'd felt earlier, and tears burned behind her lids.

Why did it feel like the early days after she'd first bolted from Witchmere? Surely she'd be done grieving a three-year-old loss, right?

Her pillow moved, scooting down, until he was facing her. Only then did Payton dare to open her eyes.

Dailey.

Staring at her with all the love she'd remembered from their bliss-filled days. But he shouldn't be there. Couldn't be. And yet...

"How are you here?" she asked in a low voice.

He tapped an invisible mask. "Tripp created it for me. It's part of my face until I leave here."

"You can't even tell it's on."

Dailey's grin was engaging. "Another perk, so I don't stand out as a stranger among Drakoryth's people."

She snorted and touched his handy-dandy breathing apparatus. "Okay, while I'm going to admit this is pretty badass, believing you don't stand out is a joke. The muffled voice is a dead giveaway."

"True."

She recalled why Vorren brought her to his home. "Did I do a lot of damage to our realm?"

"No, not at all. Our cabin will need a little shoring up, and we may need to convert the moat into a koi river, but mostly, we're good."

Our cabin.

She wanted to call him on it, but the letter needed to be addressed, *after* the surprising fact that he wasn't mauling her.

"The forced attraction doesn't affect you anymore?"

"Doesn't seem to. I mean, I'm never going to stop wanting you, but I've gone an entire thirty minutes keeping my hands to myself."

Payton nodded, choosing to ignore his comment about wanting her. People could want to fuck, but it didn't mean they were in love. And his lack of boot-inspired obsession made sense. She'd felt a change when they'd crossed the border between worlds, and the stones on her shoes hadn't lit once.

With a wiggle of her toes, she gasped. "They aren't on my feet!"

He gestured to the corner. "Seems Trickster magic doesn't work here. We were able to take them off."

"That must be why the dragons were immune back in Witchmere," she mused.

"Yeah, I believe that's the running theory."

Dailey rose and crossed to a small table. From a pitcher, he poured her a glass of water, then returned. "Drink up, Pay. As soon as you're done, we should get you to a pool or lake. At the very least, a bath."

"You and Vorren were super trusting to think I wouldn't smite you the second I woke up."

"The trust was all mine. In the end, it was his father's decree, and Vorren allowed me to stay under protest."

She snorted and drank.

"Are you ready for my heartfelt apology?" he asked softly, sinking onto the edge of the bed.

"You don't need to apologize for your feelings, Dailey—"

"Lee."

She met his earnest gaze. His offering the nickname was an olive branch of sorts, but she wasn't sure she was ready to take it.

"You don't need to apologize for your feelings," she said instead. "You made yourself clear in the letter, and your Superman complex wasn't necessary in rescuing me. I'd have returned to take my lumps when I was ready."

Dailey barely resisted the urge to hit himself on the forehead with the heel of his hand. His pigheadedness had made her wary, and rightfully so.

"Okay, one, there is no punishment awaiting you. Two, I didn't make myself clear. I muddled what I intended to say."

Payton hid behind another sip of water, remaining silent and watchful.

"I love you, Pay. I always have. The first time you looked at me with those bright, laughing eyes, my heart nearly came out of my chest. And I knew I'd never wanted anyone else." He clasped her hand, interlacing their fingers when she didn't pull away. Taking hope from her willingness to listen, he forged on. "I was a fool to write that letter without explaining why."

Her expression cooled, and she pulled away.

"I bungled everything so badly. Will you be so kind as to erase it from your mind?" he practically begged. "Please."

"If you didn't mean it, why write it?"

"It's a long story."

"We have time now that the boots are off, so to speak."

"Meaning the gloves are off? You won't fry my ass with a bolt of lightning, and I won't rain down a meteor shower?"

"Something like that. Continue."

"Our biggest problem was my mother's influence, right?" Dailey waited for the sign of her agreement before continuing. "In all of today's madness, I can't remember if I told you about the magical hold she had over me."

Although she frowned, Payton didn't interrupt, giving him a chance to explain.

"After I left you and Rowan on the sidewalk, I had an epiphany and wanted to speak with you. I was a half block away from my mother when I grew dizzy. Then I turned around, and there she was, chanting a spell."

Payton gripped his hand. "Oh my god, Lee. What was she hoping to accomplish?"

"I'm not sure. If Tripp hadn't interfered, I'm certain I wouldn't be here right now."

"What did he do?"

"He stepped between us and redirected her with a simple enchantment. But that's not all. I had Rowan sniff me—"

"You did *what?*" Payton choked out with a laugh. "I'll bet that went over well."

"Yes, she was her usual charming self. But she did confirm my mother had attached to me in some way. While normal people can't smell the effect, Rowan's wolf nose picked up her scent."

"And is this the part where you tell me Mary-Alice didn't mean to make our lives miserable?" she asked dryly.

"Not yet, but it's coming," he replied with a chuckle, lightly squeezing her fingers.

"Okay, you'd better get comfortable and tell me the rest."

Dailey explained how he'd met with Harrison and Sloane and how they'd been in contact with Flo and Brelenia. Then, he explained about the Camden curse, finishing with, "I drank Harry's potion and was able to see without blinders on for the first time. And that means seeing you for who you are to me, Wildfire. I'm able to recognize how rare our love truly is. I don't want to lose you."

"When did the letter come in?"

"After I initially met Harry and discovered what Brelenia had to say. I was worried I'd never shake my mother's influence, and I didn't want you to be miserable. How could I expect you to live the way you had when I wasn't strong enough to break free?"

He gave Payton time to process all he'd said, along with his reason for the goodbye.

"I felt horrible, Lee," she confessed. "The only thing playing on repeat in my mind was that no one loved me enough to stay in my life. I'd had years to process and come to terms with my parents' abandonment. But when it came to you, I wasn't prepared for it."

"I'm sorry for contributing to your pain, Pay. If I'd ever believed, for one second, you couldn't read the truth in my words, that it was me, not you, I'd have never written that fucking thing."

"It's a standard line when one person is trying to spare another." She shifted sideways to meet his earnest gaze. "Why not tell me in person, or better yet, hold off and not have Archer give it to me at all?"

"All I know is that we're dealing with a generational curse. We suspect it goes back almost as long as I've been alive. You don't break one of those without consequence, and I didn't want you to be part of the fallout."

Payton closed her eyes and shook her head, huffing out a frustrated breath.

Dailey's stomach soured. In his silly optimism, he'd hoped she'd understand and forgive him. "I'm sorry, Payton. More than you know," he said in a low voice, unable to manage anything louder for fear his voice would crack.

"If anything like this ever happens again, you'd better pick up a phone and call me like an adult. Got it?"

Relief made him giddy, and he grinned as he met her fierce gaze. "Is now a bad time to point out people in glass houses shouldn't throw stones?"

Her lips twisted into a grimace, and her expression grew pained.

"None of that." He tipped her chin up and tenderly kissed her. "You were right, then and now."

He laughed when she gasped in surprise.

"It should be noted that I *can* admit when I'm wrong," he teased, sobering to add, "You called it when you said I'd find a way to brush over your objections. Not because I was ignoring your concerns, but because of what's attached to my mother. I was programmed to give in to her demands."

Payton's brows dipped, and she looked like she wanted to say something, but reconsidered.

"You can always speak freely with me, Wildfire."

"You mentioned the Camdens. Are you positive they are the source? And if they are, how do you break the curse? Your mother's hatred of me runs deep, Lee. We can't dismiss that."

"We aren't positive of anything. But Mother is encased in a protective room until I can find someone strong enough to free her. As for her hatred, I'm hoping we're wrong, and she's being influenced in that area, too."

"If she isn't?" Payton asked, genuine concern reflected back at him.

He hadn't considered any other outcome or the strain it would put on their relationship. "Can we agree to cross that bridge when we get there?"

"No, Dailey. I'm not setting myself up for failure. I can't go all in if there's a chance I'll be hurt again. I won't be second best." Those eyes he loved so much glistened with unshed tears. "I can't continue to be an afterthought for everyone."

"You never will be. Your happiness is my utmost priority, Pay."

"And if we are blessed with children, she isn't allowed to make them uncomfortable with her nasty comments."

Dailey was ashamed to admit, even to himself, that he hadn't considered the weight of Payton's fears. Being a good, well-respected mother would mean everything to her. She would do the opposite of what her parents had, and she'd shower her children with all the affection she'd missed growing up. Any undermining on his mother's part would cut her to the quick.

"I choose you," he promised. "I'll always choose you first."

The first of her sobs caught him square in the chest. His own eyes stung as he held her. Together they cried as they took this healing step forward.

CHAPTER TWENTY-FIVE

Payton.

Dailey registered the warmth in his arms without ever opening his eyes as he slowly came awake.

"Hey, sleepyhead," she said, with a light kiss on his jaw. "Welcome back."

He glanced around, noting the unfamiliar space. "For a minute, I thought I'd dreamed everything, and we were in bed at our old apartment."

"I've had those dreams." The sadness in her voice was second only to the longing.

"We'll get it all back if you're willing, Pay."

She shifted to a kneeling position and pushed the hair away from her face. "I owe you an apology first."

He frowned in question.

"For trying to electrocute you," she clarified.

His inner avoidance demon wanted to brush over her

murderous tendencies, but the cop in him couldn't dismiss it as easily.

"I can't blame it all on the boots, Lee. The fury I felt was like nothing I'd experienced before."

"Why don't you tell me about it?" he suggested.

"The pain stole my breath, and I was overcome with anger." She frowned as she recalled the moment. "My father showed up, and I felt the rage building stronger. It was like the instant he said he intended to bind my powers—"

"Wait! What?" Dailey sat up, outraged on her behalf. "Why the fuck would he do that?"

"He feared the Gods putting me down like a deranged animal."

Although he could understand Rupert's motives, the timing and way the man went about it left a lot to be desired. "He should never have said that, Pay. If he had come to you with his concerns or offered it as a solution, that's one thing. But, intending to steal your magic without your consent, is bullshit."

"I thought so, too. And it was one more blow." She didn't meet his eyes and continued focusing on her wringing hand motion. "I'm not sure I'll ever feel confident in people's love for me, Lee. It's not fair to you or my parents, but I'm not sure I can trust it."

Her helplessness hurt his heart.

Dailey shifted closer, matching her kneeling position, and cupped her face. He remained that way until she found the strength to look at him.

"First, let's get this out of the way. I forgive you. I'm half convinced it's a side effect of those fucking boots." Her tentative smile warmed him. "Second, I told you I'm putting you first, and I'll spend the rest of our lives proving it. Though I want to, I can't erase your fear concerning your parents. They are going to have to show *they're* the ones worthy of your love, not the other way around."

Her smile widened, and the soft glow in her eyes felt like home. "What if I lose my shit again and try to fry your ass?"

"Meh." Dropping his arms, he shrugged. "I'm sure I'll deserve it, but I hope we never get there."

"How is Hermes?"

"I think you rewired his nervous system."

She paled.

"I'm kidding, Pay. He was on his way to full recovery when I left to find you."

"Maybe my father was right. Maybe my power should be bound. What if I had killed Hermes? Zeus would've declared war on Witchmere."

He didn't hesitate. He didn't believe there was any need to neutralize her as a threat. "Elara has learned control, and if you'd have hung around, Tripp would've made sure you were as advanced as she is. If you intend to stick this time, we'll get you the training you require to maintain balance," he promised.

"I'm staying if you'll have me back."

"I'm more than willing."

"Can you forgive me for running away? Can you fully trust me?"

Forgiveness was easy. He already had. Trust was harder, and his indecision must've shown.

"You can't," she whispered, pressing her hands to her stomach.

He recognized the action as her feeling insecure and alone in her worry.

"I told you I understand why you left. With understanding comes forgiveness, Pay. Trusting that you'll not leave again is a helluva lot harder, but I'm working through it. Can that be enough?"

"I don't want to feel like I have something to prove every day," she said achingly. "I can't keep doing that. It's been lifelong as it is."

"You don't have to prove shit." His tone was emphatic, and he meant it. "The problem is on my side. I'll grow comfortable as our communication grows. And before you say it, I know you tried. I wasn't able to hear you before." He held out his hand to her. "Can you trust I'll listen with an open heart? Can you believe I want to resolve our differences and make your happiness a priority? Trust goes both ways."

Placing her hand in his, she nodded. "I can."

"Good. Ready to head back and slay the dragon?"

The building rumbled, and they both froze.

"Is this place alive?" he asked in a whisper.

The bed shook.

"I guess I have my answer," he muttered. Raising his voice, he called out, "My blunder was a figure of speech. There will be zero dragon slaying. We like dragons. They're welcome anytime they want to visit our realm."

Laughter danced in Payton's eyes, and she covered her mouth to smother a giggle.

"Yeah, you have nothing to worry about. I still have to walk outside and face an angry hoard, if this building decides to tell on me."

A pillow rose up and smacked him in the face.

"I think that's your punishment and reminder to watch your tongue," she said with a grin.

"Okay. New rules: no dragon slaying, no lightning bolt throwing, no running away, and absolutely not pretending problems don't exist," he said, ticking off points with his fingers. "Did I miss anything?"

"Nope."

"Let's go."

Casting a regretful look across the room, she said, "I have to put on the boots to go back."

"What? Why? Can't we conjure new shoes?"

"I don't think so. We must resolve this to the Trickster's satisfaction."

"We just did," he argued, as panic crept in.

"But not in our world."

As she slid them onto her feet, he couldn't erase his apprehension. What would happen when they crossed the threshold to their plane? Would he feel compelled to objectify her again? Goddess, he hoped not! Walking around with a hard-on and no thought but copulation was as painful as it was embarrassing.

They traversed the corridors, following the direction of the staff, to find Vorren and see if they could hitch a ride back to Witchmere. Like Dailey, Payton had hated the idea of shoving her feet in those devil boots. Yet the compulsion rose up. Unfortunately, she could also understand the logic behind the urge.

Their personal trials weren't over until the Trickster

magic said it was. She only hoped these damned things weren't insulted over her attack on Hermes.

Dailey gave her hand a light squeeze. "You okay?"

"Yes. I was just wondering if the boots will require restitution from me for hurting their master."

He stopped walking, tugging her to a halt. His complexion was ashen. "Christ! We can't go back until we know. I'm not risking your safety."

Stretching up, she kissed him, then patted his chest where his badge should be.

"Always the protector."

"I'm serious, Pay."

"We have to," she countered, scrunching her nose in distaste for what was to come. "It's the only way to get our lives back and end the madness associated with the enchantment."

He swore savagely.

"It'll be okay, Lee. I promise."

She wasn't sure how she knew, but she did. Or maybe she was just that determined to straighten her shit out.

Vorren came upon them hugging. "Ah! All is well with your mating, yes?"

"We never had a problem 'mating,'" Dailey retorted. "But yes, she no longer feels the need to eviscerate me."

"Must be that he is good with the mating, despite being puny." Vorren grinned and shot Payton a wink, and she did her damnedest not to laugh. "You are for home now?" he asked.

"If we can catch a ride," she replied, raising her brows to stress the point.

"Of course. I must find my remaining eggs. Corvack has

assured me he will continue the search. I had promised my wife…" A pained expression crossed his visage before he looked away. "Are you ready to leave now, or would you prefer to break your fast?"

"Food would be wonderful." During the night, someone had been kind enough to leave them a tray of fruit and refill their water pitcher, but Dailey had to be ready to chew off his arm about now.

Vorren led them down two flights of marbled stairs to the dining room.

"What is your plan when you return to Witchmere?" he asked as he directed them to their chairs.

She shared a glance with Dailey. "We've worked through a lot last night and today. The hope is the Trickster's magical boots will recognize the progress we've made and ease their destructive tendencies."

"And we need to remove the Triad's spell from my family, so we don't go through this again," he added.

Vorren frowned. "What is this… Triad? Are they a threat to my children? I shall be happy to vanquish them for you, Law Dog."

Payton barely held back another laugh at his eagerness and Dailey's resulting frustrated expression. As an officer, he believed in a specific code, one that didn't include random enemy vanquishing for sport.

"While I appreciate the offer, Highness, I'm going to do my best to take care of this the legal way."

The conversation remained light for the remainder of their meal, and an hour later, they were flying through the veil toward the cabin. With the exception of Nazek, the place appeared deserted.

"Greetings!" He called from his seat on the porch swing. The wood and chains strained under his weight as he stood to join them.

"Remind me to reinforce that overhang," Dailey said in an aside.

She was about to reply when the difference in his behavior registered. In her rage, she'd missed then what was obvious today.

"Lee?"

His brows shot up in question.

"Are you feeling particularly amorous?"

With a roguish grin, he swept her into his arms. "Why? Are you? Because if you are, I'm happy to satisfy all your needs."

But other than holding her, he didn't act out of the ordinary by showering her with kisses or attempting to get her naked. She glanced at her feet and would swear the boots winked at her.

"Pay?"

"You're not, um, overcome?"

"I—oh!" He laughed. "No. And I have a theory about it."

"Care to share, Law Dog?" Vorren asked.

Dailey's mouth tightened, likely to hold back a sarcastic retort. Without replying to Dragon Daddy, he led her into the cabin, shutting out the others.

"Yesterday, you didn't feel wanted. Today, you know you are."

"That doesn't explain why you were back to normal around the time of my temper tantrum," she pointed out.

"Actually, it does." She frowned, unable to make the connection, and he went on to explain, "You'd closed off your heart and were focused on the injustice of being rejected. You weren't concentrating on your feelings of inadequacy."

A light switched on. "The boots are contrary fuckers. My desire to be wanted and loved was snuffed out, so there was nothing to amplify other than my self-righteous fury," she concluded.

The diamonds put on a light show.

"Bingo." A wicked smile curled his lips. "Do you suppose I'm allowed to show you just how much you are loved, wanted, and desired?"

An answering heat burned low in her belly, and she groaned her frustration. "As much as I wish I could say yes, we can't risk it until these things are gone."

"Fair. Why don't we have the pyro lizards escort us to town, and make sure the villagers don't head your way?"

He turned toward the door.

"Lee?"

Seeing her hesitation, he returned to her. "What is it, Pay?"

"I've made peace with Flo, my mother, and you. I'm also working through my self-doubt. What do you think is left?"

"Maybe there's nothing left for you. Maybe it's me, or a challenge for us as a couple," he suggested.

Tingling started in her toes. "I believe you're right, or as close as can be."

He held out his hand. "Ready?"

CHAPTER TWENTY-SIX

After directing Vorren and Nazek where to meet them, Dailey and Payton teleported to Elara's old apartment.

"It's now or never," she said, preparing to test her seductive siren charms. If still active, they needed to hightail it back to the cabin. Though Dailey wouldn't be heartbroken to be there alone with her. They hadn't had any true privacy except at Drakoryth's Castle.

He experienced a slight trepidation when she unlocked the slider and opened the door, but he shoved his anxiety aside. Together, they stepped out on the porch overlooking town.

Dailey was struck by how little time had passed since he attempted to arrest her and that exact second. Christmas was still days away, and tourists crowded the sidewalks of Main Street. Festive music floated up, and from their spot, they could see the three-story tree decked out in all its holiday finery.

Payton sighed. "I love this view."

"Me, too."

His condo was across the thoroughfare, diagonal to this one. Unfortunately, it didn't boast the unobstructed views of town. Although he'd had opportunities, he hadn't upgraded. As to why, he'd freely admit to being a sentimental fool. There, he felt closer to Payton than anywhere else. If they eventually decide to move forward together as a couple, it might be best to get rid of anything tying them to their old relationship.

"Isn't that Doctor Weatherspoon waving at us?" With a frown, Payton leaned farther over the rail. "Does she seem frantic to you?"

"She does." Dailey eased her away from the edge and dropped a soft, lingering kiss on her lips. "I'll see what she wants and be right back. Please stay here. If things turn weird, head back to the cabin."

"I'm going with you."

"Pay—"

Gripping his jaw, she turned his face toward the street. "What do you see, Lee?"

"A very fucking crowded town and danger lurking around every corner."

She laughed. "Yes, to the first part, and no, to the second. You're paranoid now."

"Okay, I give up. What am I missing?"

"The shifters are going about their business. They haven't stopped to sniff the air, and no one but your doctor friend is trying to get our attention." She grinned. "Archer is resting atop the building across from us, with Cecil and Greer on the adjoining rooftops."

He scanned their surroundings with a practiced eye.

"You're right. The dragon brothers are lounging in the doorways on either side of the entrance."

"I'm safe, Lee."

Her excitement was contagious, and he chuckled at her happy dance.

"All right. Let's go meet with Hope."

She flagged them down as they exited the lobby. "Lee! Payton!"

Although Payton frowned, she didn't remark on the use of the nickname, and he was grateful she decided to let it slide.

"What's going on, Hope?" he asked

"I overheard my mother and my Uncle Orson—" she began.

"Orson?" he cut in sharply. "Orson Camden? He's your uncle?"

Today, of all days, it was too much of a coincidence. Because of their prior intimacy, finding out she was a Camden felt like a betrayal of sorts. Why hadn't she told him?

Eyes wide and wary, Hope appeared taken aback by his aggression. "Yes. My mother is his twin sister, Ophelia. I'm sorry. I thought you knew."

"I don't recall you ever mentioning it."

"Camden?" Payton asked, her eyes widening as she made the connection.

"Yes. Why are you both acting like you're hearing the name for the first time?" Hope asked, her bewilderment showing. "My family has been here for generations."

"It doesn't matter," he replied. He fell back on his police

training, determined not to reveal what he knew. At the same time, he had to be smart and pry information out of her. "What's this about your mother and uncle?"

"They were discussing your mother, Lee." Her expression reflected her worry. "I think they are planning to use her in some way. They dropped your name, too, but I can't be sure of what I overheard."

"Start from the top. What was said?" he asked, suppressing his alarm.

"They began arguing after Mother said she hadn't been able to locate Mary-Alice. She claimed she had scryed in addition to using a location spell." She wrung her hands. "She narrowed your Mother's whereabouts to this block and told Uncle Orson she intended to start searching at the town square. I don't have a good feeling about this, Lee. We must get to her first."

"Fuck!" He heaved a sigh. Yes, the Triad problem existed, but he'd hoped to have more time before shit blew up in his face. "Okay, I'll take it from here. Thanks."

Her agitation grew with every word he spoke, and he felt like a total dick for his suspicions. She shivered before casting a glance behind her and freezing in place.

Following her gaze, Dailey spotted Orson Camden heading their way. His visage was a mask of barely controlled violence.

"Payton, take Hope upstairs."

"No time." She moved in front of them and raised her arms at the exact instant green mist rose from the sidewalk grates, encircling them.

He swore as he reached for her, but she sidestepped.

"*Incapsulare!*" she called out.

A clear, full-body gel-like substance coated him from head to toe. The instant panic associated with not breathing shot through him, and he struggled against the fear. Succumbing and losing his mind would only make things worse. Yet despite his logic, his body had other ideas, forcing him to claw at his face. Unable to hold his breath another second, he gasped. The surprise came in the form of air to his lungs, and he greedily drank it in.

Hope was in a similar state, and in her frantic mindset, she tore at her protective covering.

"You can breathe," he shouted to her, praying the sound would carry to her.

Orson reached them, halting in front of Payton. His ruddy complexion was more flushed than usual. Promised retribution was there in his beady eyes.

Dailey fought like hell to get to them, but the most minute movement was like running in water against the current, and he couldn't gain traction. Helpless, he could only stand aside while the coming drama played out.

"You foolish girl!" Orson snarled. "You've ruined everything! Why couldn't you stay gone?"

Payton crossed her arms and tapped her toe. Her expression was one of cool indifference. "What did I ruin, you naked mole rat?"

In fairness to her, the man *did* resemble a naked mole with his squinty eyes and odd-shaped bald head. He wasn't overly tall, leaning toward short and stout, with stubby arms and splayed fingers. His cherry-red nose was long, yet pointy and upturned on the end.

Dailey curbed his desire to laugh. Leave it to Payton to point out what others missed.

"You dare!" Orson sputtered.

"Yep, quite a bit," she said with a bored study of her nails.

She ignored the poisonous gas rising around her. Right as Dailey's worry for her reached a fever pitch, the diamonds on her shoes flickered to life. The mist reversed course, weaving around Orson and inching ever higher.

Was he wrong? Had Payton been the one to create the toxin? Dailey immediately rejected the notion.

From down the block, a woman cried out. "Orson, no!"

But it was too late, and the mist had closed around his throat, choking him.

Vorren and Nazek appeared on either side of Dailey like magical mob enforcers. "You want we should stop this?" The only thing missing was the New York street thug accent.

Hermes stepped from the shadows, and a mere twirl of his finger put Orson in a trance-like state. To Vorren, he said, "You can return to your Easter egg hunt, Pyro. I've got this one."

"Better send Tripp after this guy's sister," Payton replied, tipping her chin in the direction of Orphelia. "She took off as soon as Dragon Daddy joined us."

"She's not who we're after. It's the other two members of the Triad who have been a bit more elusive."

Payton nodded as she snapped her fingers. His protective gel shell dissolved into a puddle of clear liquid at Dailey's feet, and Hope's soon followed.

As soon as he was free, he stormed over and wrapped Paton in a bear hug.

"Don't do that again," he ordered in a low voice. "My heart can't take it."

She smiled and patted his chest. "You have to ask your-self, which of the two of us can withstand toxic air?"

"Valid, but how did you know it was imminent?"

Frowning, she shook her head. "I'm not exactly sure. Maybe it's the same way Hermes can sense I'm in trouble?"

"It's atmospheric change, Sergeant Straightlace," the Trickster explained. "Gods—and Titans—are attuned to minuscule anomalies in their environment. It's instinctive. Our sixth sense kicks in, and we shift into a natural protective mode for those we care about."

"But that's not always the case," Payton argued. "There have been many times the deities haven't bothered to intervene."

"Gods are big on mortals learning lessons," he replied with a careless shrug. Turning to Hope, he asked, "Why would your family want Payton out of the way?"

She appeared adorably confused. "How would I know?"

"I think I do," Dailey said slowly. As the reason took shape in his mind, he became sure of it. "They wanted Payton out of the way so I could marry Hope."

"Me?" Hope gasped.

"A Camdon-Cobb union!" Payton exclaimed. "It would be a splendid merging of the town's most powerful families." She shot him a laughing glance from beneath her lashes. "I'm surprised Mary-Alice didn't break a hip jumping up and down in her joy at the idea of Hope as a daughter-in-law."

"That makes no sense. Everyone knows he loves you," Hope protested.

"Not everyone." He grimaced. "There are those convinced absence doesn't make the heart fonder, and they went about feeding my bitterness."

"So that if I returned, you'd hate me," Payton said softly, her eyes regretful. "I'm so sorry I made you a target, Lee."

"You didn't. They, however, made a grave error." He tucked a strand of her hair behind her ear, stroking the delicate shell in the process. "I would never marry anyone but you, Wildfire. Their hopes for a union between Hope and me were in vain."

"Gee, thanks." But the good doctor didn't appear broken up by his comment. In fact, she looked amused.

Payton snorted, and she cast a laughing glance Hope's way. "Neither of you was willing, though I'm sure you may have gotten there had all his emotions been intact. Right?"

"Probably." Hope wry smile was self-directed. Stretching on tiptoe, she kissed Dailey's cheek. "Be happy, Lee." She shifted back toward Payton. "I still expect a girls' night with margaritas now that you'll be hanging around."

"I never claimed I was," Payton protested, and Dailey's heart stalled until she added, "But the first round is on you, Doc."

"We'll charge it to my Camden credit card. Restitution on their behalf." Sincerity shone in her coppery gaze. "I'm sorry for all the grief my family has caused you both. Please don't hesitate to call if I can do anything to make up for their poor behavior."

Dailey shared a look with Payton and Hermes. He wasn't prepared to let her go without a clear warning regarding what the perpetrators would face for their crimes, regardless of connection.

"I get that they're your family, Hope, but they can't go around dominating people, rearranging outcomes to suit them as they have."

"I know. They're focused on dynastic greatness." She shook her head. "For them, it's all about advantageous unions. Their ambition and desire for excess wealth far surpass any morals they may have once had."

"Can you tell us what we're dealing with here, or how to break their hold?"

"I wish I could. If I uncover anything, I'll contact you right away." She'd taken four steps before backtracking. "I recall my mother once discussed a maze of tunnels under Witchmere. It was back when I was a child. Maybe ten or twelve. I wouldn't swear to it, but I'm pretty sure the basement under the Camden Investment building interconnects with them all."

Tingling started along Dailey's spine. "Like the one under City Hall."

"There is a tunnel throughway under us?" Payton's eyes lit with interest, and she eyed the buildings around them. "I wonder how many of these places open into it?"

"All of them," answered the gravelly voice of Archer Roche. He approached, adding, "Every last one has a hidden passageway. It was how we, the magical residents, traversed prior to the charming of alleyways."

"Clever," Hope murmured, casting him a smile. "Maybe you'd like to go for coffee one day, and you can tell me more about this place."

His smile was noncommittal.

Dailey imagined Archer's lack of interest had to do with Rowan's sister, Katie. More than once, he'd caught the gargoyle sending her pining glances. The guy consumed a helluva lot of soup from her shop, *Serendipity*, for a man of his muscular stature.

"The clan and I will find the Camdens if they emerge from their underground lair," Archer promised. Dailey could swear the man's eye twitched as he suggested the alternative. "You can always see if those overgrown lizards will hunt below. They are little better than sewer rats and may have an advantage."

So saying he disappeared as soundlessly as he arrived.

"He's already taken, isn't he?" Hope said with a defeated sigh. "My radar is broken, and I always pick the unavailable ones."

Hermes flashed her a grin. "I am—"

"Don't go there," Dailey warned, cutting him off. "You'll get a story, a rash, and regret. In no particular order."

With a good-natured laugh, the Trickster gestured to Orson. "Where is the best holding cell for his kind?"

"Follow me."

CHAPTER TWENTY-SEVEN

Payton bided her time as Dailey and Hermes walked away with Orson Camden in tow, then faced Hope.

"Okay, tell me what you really know."

"I—"

"See these boots?" She waited for the doctor to look and nod. "They're a human lie detector, and something has been off with you for the last few minutes. What's going on?"

"Ever since Dailey pointed out the potential Camden-Cobb connection, I couldn't help thinking about Sloane's husband, Bradford. I think he's in on it, too."

Sensing Hope's honesty, Payton considered the best way to bring it up to the Cobbs. Perhaps it was her ability as a doctor to see below the surface, but Hope picked up on her dilemma.

"I had the same problem, Payton. I wanted to mention it to Dailey, but if Brad's not involved, it could ruin his relationship with his wife."

"Is he in town?" She might be able to find him and confront him if he were.

"Not that I'm aware of."

As if their conversation summoned her, Sloane exited Harrison's office building and headed straight for them. "Ladies. Have you seen my brother?"

"He's escorting Orson Camden to jail."

There was an underlying restlessness about Dailey's sister, and her nervous energy was leeching out, creating trepidation within Payton. Hope seemed tuned in to it, too, and she studied them curiously as if seeking the cause.

The combined nervousness set Payton's teeth on edge. "What's going on, Sloane?"

"If you've been with Dailey, he's probably told you about the situation with our mother." She paused for confirmation before saying, "Mother's been slipping in and out of consciousness for the last couple of hours. Harrison is convinced she shouldn't have been contained as long as she has."

Although Payton already suspected it, she had to ask, "Whose spell is holding her?"

"D's."

"If I release her, what happens? She goes back to trying to control everything again?"

"We can't let her go, Pay. She's dangerous, especially to you and Dailey. I don't think she'll stop trying to run you out of town until she's succeeded."

"Dailey's not strong enough to remove the Triad's spell. That leaves me, Hermes, or Tripp."

"What about me?" Hope suggested. "I'm half Camden by blood. Is there a way I can help reverse the damage?"

"I haven't trained properly since coming into my abilities. Whatever I ultimately do could get you hurt, Hope." Old insecurities tried to choke Payton, and she shook out her hands, hoping to dispel the sensation.

Ever the perceptive one, Sloane asked, "Are you okay, Pay?"

"Yes." The old adage 'fake it 'til you make it' came to mind. She reached for her phone and swore when she came up empty-handed. "May I use your cell?"

After unlocking hers, Sloane passed it to Payton.

She punched in her sister's number and exhaled her relief as soon as Elara answered. Asking for help went against her nature, but if it meant ensuring the Cobb family's safety, she'd do it.

A stone flared brightly on her shoes, and by her count, she was close to ticking off all the boxes on their to-do list.

Elara, as always, was immediately concerned for her welfare. "Pay? Are you all right?"

"Peachy keen. Can you meet me at Harrison's office? Like now?"

"I'll be there in a flash."

As the three of them crossed the road, light flared through the upstairs window before dimming.

"She wasn't kidding," Payton muttered.

Her sister greeted her with a quick searching glance and a hug. "What's this about?"

"Can we combine our power to remove the spell haunting Mary-Alice?"

Elara's blonde brows shot up. "Why would you want to? Don't you hate her?"

Sloane choked, but there was a distinct laugh behind the sound.

With an exasperated glare at the group, Payton said, "I don't hate her. I don't hate *anybody*." Across the distance, she met Mary-Alice's haughty stare. "But I don't necessarily love how bitchy she is. Now, knowing it may not be her fault... I actually feel sorry for her."

Her words had a sobering effect on Sloane. Her expression was stricken, and she'd turned ashen.

Lowering her voice, Payton said, "I'm sorry if she was awful to you. Dailey told me a little bit, but he didn't want to betray confidences."

"It's okay."

"Are you ready for us to attempt this?"

Sloane nodded and shot her brother an inquiring glance. "Any objections, Harry?"

"I'm not convinced it's a simple reversal," he said. Gesturing for them to join him at the desk, he tapped various pages he'd photocopied from a grimoire. "There's a similar spell in our family's book. But it's a 'once done, cannot be undone' enchantment."

"How do you know it's the same?" his sister asked.

"Here." He shuffled a few papers and ran a finger under each sentence as he read off the list of effects. "The primary one is the mist, which is only visible when it faces strong opposition. Like with Mother earlier."

"And with us in the street," Hope added. "Is it possible, as a Camden, that I can help?"

"Every indication states it would need a blood sacrifice," he replied, far too serious for Payton's state of mind.

Harrison didn't do extremes. Maybe it was his profession, but the guy was as laid back and steady as they came.

"Whose?" Payton dreaded the answer. The little voice in the back of her mind was screaming at her, asking why the hell she'd even brought it up.

"The ultimate targets."

"But that could be anyone! Sloane, Brad, Hope, and…" She couldn't bring herself to say Dailey's name. The solution, with his death being the only way to end this madness, was unfathomable. "Okay. What about a transference? Could we do that? Split it between a few people? I'll volunteer as tribute." Even suggesting it made her queasy, but she firmed her resolve. Saving Dailey was the key.

"Who would be willing to take on that sort of curse?" His tone said the suggestion was beyond ridiculous and that the entire thing was hopeless.

"I would," Hope said, beating her to it. "You could transfer it to me."

Goddess, bless her meddlesome heart!

"You're the wrong Camden. It's the others who deserve to be punished," Sloane replied. Her sour tone was a clear indicator of trouble in paradise. But then, Payton had always questioned the woman's sanity when it came to marrying the Bougie Brad. Sloane's understated classiness was miles above that pretentious douche canoe.

"The wrong Camden…" Harrison murmured.

A Eureka moment hit them all at once, and they shared an *oh-my-God* glance.

"If no one is going to say it, I will." Payton grinned, perhaps a little too wickedly. "We'll turn it back on them."

"I love it." Sloane laughed.

They were only minutes into formulating a plan when the hallway door swung open, revealing Dailey, Hermes, and Tripp.

Payton was practically buzzing when she approached him. "Lee, we have a fabul—"

He shook his head. "It won't work."

"You didn't hear what I have to say."

"My mother did," Tripp said, his mouth turning down. "She's been watching everything like a damned soap opera through her scrying mirror." He held up his phone. "I got her call and rushed right over."

"Well, then what the hell are we supposed to do?" Payton snapped.

"We're working on it." On cue, Dailey's phone pinged, and he glanced at the screen. "All set."

"All set for what?"

He closed his eyes, tilted his head back.

"Dailey?"

FWOOOOOOOSH—FWOOOOOOOSH!

The thundering booms shook their building. Shouting from the street signaled Dailey's successful bombing of City Hall. His meteor summoning had come in handy.

As one, their group surged to the bank of windows.

Payton was the first to confront him. "Lee? Oh my god! What did you do?"

The accusation in her eyes stung, but she wasn't in on the plan yet.

"What I had to. No one was close to the building," he assured her. "Tripp and Hermes implanted a mass suggestion, rushing everyone to the square for an impromptu Christmas concert. Junior texted to say the building was clear."

"But why?"

"Because until my mother is well, she can't be in charge of Witchmere." He crossed to Payton and tipped up her chin. "It was the only way, Wildfire."

"I believe you, but how the hell do we explain all this? People will ask."

"We'll tell them she was injured in the freak accident and was taken to our family estate to heal. The town will elect a new mayor, one not under Camden's rule, allowing us time to find a solution."

"But—"

He tried to rein in his impatience, but he had to do damage control and didn't have time for the third degree. "I have to go, Pay. What will it look like if the Chief of Police isn't on scene?"

"Okay. What do you want the rest of us to do?"

He fucking loved her willingness to help, whatever her objection. Leaning in, he kissed her.

"Thank you."

"For what?"

"For being you. And to answer your question, Hermes and Tripp will take my mother to the Cobb estate, where Greer and Cecil will keep guard until a workable solution can be found." He grinned at Harrison. "We can't keep her here. Our dear Harry has a backlog of patients to treat."

"Who knew Witchmere was a breeding ground for hot messes?" Payton quipped.

Everyone raised a hand.

Dailey crossed to Mary-Alice. Dread curled inside him for her anticipated reaction.

"All tunnel access to the main house will be cut off. You'll be quarantined there until we can help you."

She hissed her disproval.

"It won't be long," he said. "We'll free you of this curse, Mother."

"You fool!" she spat, surprising everyone when she broke through the containment wards and wrapped her hands around his throat.

Her responding fury was expected, and Dailey did nothing to stop her. If those fucking Camdens required a sacrifice, he'd gladly give it to save Sloane and, eventually, Harrison.

"*STOP!*" Payton bellowed.

The grandfather clock against the back wall ceased mid-pendulum swing.

Payton jerked his motionless mother's hand from his neck, shoved her onto the chair, and smothered her in gel. Then, with a wave of her hand, she released everyone from their frozen state.

"Are you fucking mental?" Payton snapped at him. "She intended to kill you!"

Dailey remained silent, letting her draw her own conclusions. Horror transformed her visage, as her fury was suspended.

"That was your intent." She breathed in sharply. "Lee. *Why?*"

The agony in her voice broke his damned heart.

"They're my kid sister and brother, Pay," he said achingly. "I can't let the Triad or my mother ruin their lives. Not like they used me and tried to destroy ours. Can't you understand?"

She nodded, but her eyes told a different story. Inside, she felt betrayed that he'd made the split-second decision without discussing it first.

"Most of all, I did it for you," he added. "I won't let you suffer her verbal abuse anymore. I told you I wouldn't allow her to control our lives, and I meant it."

"Why couldn't you trust us to find a solution together? One that didn't end with you six feet under?"

Her boots lit, and with sudden clarity, he knew he fucked up royally this time. Closing his eyes, he hung his head. He'd be lucky if she ever talked to him after this.

The silence stretched until he thought he'd go mad. When he peeked, she was still there, waiting.

"I thought you were going to leave, right then. I couldn't watch you go," he admitted. "Not again."

"I'm not leaving you, Dailey James Cobb. If you want me gone, it's going to take a shitload more effort on your part." Her determination and commitment were in the firm set of her jaw and the assurance in her eyes. "No matter how long it takes, or how ugly she is to me, I'm sticking."

He wasn't aware he was crying until she brushed the moisture from his cheeks.

"I made a promise to you at Drakoryth. You'll always be my number-one priority. Come hell or high water, I'm keeping it," he said roughly.

Elara stomped over to Hermes and socked him in the arm. "It's a wrap."

"Right! Sounds like vows to me, too!" He crowed with a

resounding clap. Payton's burgundy boots appeared in his arms.

With an audible gasp, she peered at her bare feet.

"What happened?" Dailey asked, bewildered.

"You fulfilled their requirements, Sergeant Statute," the Trickster said, gracing them with a warm smile. With lightning-fast speed, he removed the largest jewel and reworked it into a pendant, nestling it among a circle of rubies. Then he handed it to Payton with a flourish. "For you, my dear. A gift to remember me by."

Elara rolled her eyes. "He says that to all the boots' victims."

"Ah, but they never forget me," he countered smugly.

"Because you're a cautionary tale," Dailey said, drawing Payton into his arms. "No giant asteroids on the horizon."

"No townful or beachful of people hoping to bang me."

"Beachful?"

"Remind me to tell you about the army of Merpeople." She wrapped her arms around his neck with a laugh. "But I must say, some of those men were quite impressive."

"So what you're telling me is that all our vacations are going to take place inland from here on out," he replied, pressing his forehead to hers. They shared a sigh of relief.

"We'll take care of Mayor Murder," Hermes assured them.

"It's good to know I'm not the only one he makes up names for," Dailey muttered.

"But I'll always have a special reserve for you, Officer Ordinance."

EPILOGUE

ONE YEAR LATER...

Christmas Day dawned bright and beautiful. The golden rays streamed through the cabin's skylight, caressing Payton's blonde hair and giving her an angelic air.

Dailey grinned.

He knew it to be false. Last night, she'd been a wild, wanton goddess—no enchanted boots needed.

"Stop staring at me. It's creepy," she said in a husky voice.

"It's my favorite pastime. Ready to get up and face the day?"

"No."

Typical Payton.

"Has anyone ever told you how ornery you are in the mornings?" he teased.

She peeked one bleary eye open, and he felt the heat from her glare.

In response, he held up a perfectly flavored, steaming cup of coffee.

"You thoughtful sonofabitch," she muttered as she sat up and shoved her hair back. "Gimme."

"Scooch over, bed hog."

After she made room for him, Dailey handed her the mug.

"Do you know what today is?"

With a scrunch of her nose and a squint of one eye, she shook her head.

He laughed. "Liar."

"Why are you still here? Isn't it bad luck to see the bride on her wedding day?"

"That's for the groom, and I'm under strict orders from Tripp to get Elara to the venue on time." He kissed her temple. "He's worried she'll bolt. Apparently, there's a rumor going around about the Hawthorne sisters being runaway brides."

"Okay, that was one time. Poor El can't be tainted by association." She sipped her drink. "Damn, Lee. I think this is the best cup yet."

"You say that every morning," he replied dryly.

"And I mean it!"

"You have one hour, then I'm coming back. If you're not ready, there will be hell to pay."

"What can be worse than global extinction from super volcanoes and asteroids?" she asked with an eye roll.

"Brelenia's wrath."

"Fair point." She handed off her mug, kissed him, then tumbled from the bed.

"You're so graceful," he quipped, leaning sideways to admire her bare ass.

"Shut it, Officer Knob. Or no more of this"—she slapped her butt cheek—"later."

Laughter bubbled up in his chest, and he set the coffee aside.

He lunged for her as she made a run for the bathroom and locked herself inside.

"Game on, Hawthorne! Game on!"

Her muffled giggle made him grin, and he paused to let his happiness settle.

The last year hadn't been easy.

After a few therapy sessions, he and Payton had forged new bonds. He'd rented out their old condo and purchased the building housing Elara's old apartment. They planned to renovate all four floors and expand into the empty lot behind the original structure. Permits had been harder to obtain due to the stricter rules imposed by Witchmere's new mayor, Archer Roche. Apparently, he liked the architecture as it was. Thankfully, he had a soft spot for Katie Sanderson, and Payton hadn't been above using it.

Construction was moving right along, and 98% of their tenants had placed down payments on their future condos. Of course, it helped that Dailey was a warlock and could keep maintenance dues at a bare minimum. It required little magic or effort to keep the place in tip-top condition.

The Triad's curse was an ongoing challenge, though, and they were still dealing with the fallout. But honestly, he was thrilled Sloane had left Bradford the Bougie Biscuit, and he'd made no bones about telling her. But the Camden elders would get theirs soon. He'd see to it.

The bathroom door opened, and Payton paused in the opening.

The effect stole his breath.

She was a vision, and he thanked his lucky stars every fucking day. When they were old and gray, he'd still be grateful. Because she was his everything, his reason for existing.

"Lee." Her voice was too serious, and his heart began to hammer painfully. "Before we go, can we talk?"

The tone and "talk" reference were never a great combination, and he did his damnedest not to wince. He'd promised to always listen and keep their lines of communication open, and by the Goddess, that's exactly what he'd do. He only hoped he didn't hate the outcome.

"Of course. What is it, Pay?"

"Will you sit down on the bed, please?"

Once he was settled, she opened the nightstand drawer and removed a small box.

His heart stalled.

He recognized it as the one he'd held during his proposal. "Payton?"

Instead of answering, she eased up the hem of her bridesmaid gown and knelt before him. Holding out her hand, she cleared her throat. Her fingers shook as she flipped the lid of the box open.

Centered inside, beside the ring he'd given her, was its male counterpart. The band was platinum with an etched design, familiar yet not. His mind struggled to recall while simultaneously trying to wrap itself around her actions. The memory surfaced. It was a protection spell for the wearer.

"I love you, Dailey. And if you're still willing to build a future together, I'm asking you to marry me. Will you?"

His throat was too thick to speak, so he joined her on

the floor. Kneeling in front of her, he removed the box from her trembling grasp and withdrew her old ring. For the longest moment, he was caught by the single winking solitaire.

"Are you in love with this design?" he asked.

"What?" She was adorable in her confusion.

"It's a solitaire, but it seems lonely. I was thinking it should be surrounded by stones that loved it," he replied, capturing and holding her stare.

A blissful smile transformed her face, and he once again struggled to draw a breath. "Yes, I think it needs the love of another to shine the way it's supposed to."

He drew the magic from his core, then brushed his fingers over the setting, creating the new setting as he imagined it.

"May I?" he asked. When she nodded, he slid the ring home.

Her hum of appreciation was his reward. Just as it always was.

Then, she picked up the discarded box and removed his ring.

"You didn't answer me," she said pertly. "Dailey James Cobb, will you marry me?"

"I did answer. You weren't listening." Leaning forward, he took her hand in his and helped her slide his ring in place. They spent only a moment admiring it before he swept her up and kissed her. "I will marry you every day for the rest of our lives, Payton Hawthorne, if that's what it takes to make you as happy as you make me."

"Every day seems excessive, but I'm not opposed to the occasional vow renewal." A naughty smile curled her lush mouth. "I think we still have thirty minutes before we have to get Elara to the clearing."

"Hm. What did you have in mind?"

"Something very wanton. You in?"

He conjured a pair of handcuffs. "Are we doing this the easy way or the hard way?"

Rand held out his hand, palm up. "Give them to me."

"Rand, darling—"

"Brelenia, we are never going through that again. Give me the damned boots. I intend to see they're destroyed."

She crinkled her nose. "There's just one small hitch with your plan, my love."

He crossed his arms, pleased to see her lick her lips as her gaze lingered on his muscled chest.

"You were saying?" he asked

"I was?" she sounded delightfully confused.

But it was a partial act. He'd been married to the woman for centuries and knew all of her stall tactics.

"The boots, Brel. I want them out of commission."

She huffed in frustration. "Fine. Top shelf on the left," she said with a gesture toward her walk-in wardrobe. "But they won't stay hidden, Rand. Those blasted things have a life of their own."

"Then maybe our resident pain in the ass needs a taste of his own medicine."

Brelenia's eyes lit up. "Tripp had mentioned the same thing. Perhaps it's time to bring Hermes and Storm Bringer together. What do you say?"

Rand halted halfway to the closet.

The idea had merit.

Knowing he'd probably live to regret it, he agreed.

Thank you for reading Wanton Witchmas. If you'd be so kind as to write an honest review, I'd be forever grateful.

Turn the page to see what else I'm brewing!

WHAT'S NEXT...

THE TRAVELER book 4 in the Sentinels of Magic series, is right after that. It's the story of Alexander Castor that everyone's been waiting for.

Expected Release: May 2026

I'm also hard at work on a new series, ***Angels of Legend***, and I hope to kick it off this spring with ***LUCIFER***. Many of you have preordered from my shop, and I'm sure you'll be excited to learn it's 50% completed. While I hesitate to make promises, I hope to have it done by mid-April 2026. Please check back for retailer links!

*If you think you may have ordered it but aren't sure, please feel free to email me, tmc@tmcromer.com, or log in to your **TM CROMER BOOKS** shop account to view your purchase history.

https://tmcromer.shop

BOOKS BY T.M. CROMER

Get your printable list [here](#)!

PARANORMAL ROMANCE

The Thorne Witches®:
SUMMER MAGIC
AUTUMN MAGIC
WINTER MAGIC
SPRING MAGIC
REKINDLED MAGIC
LONG LOST MAGIC
FOREVER MAGIC
ESSENTIAL MAGIC
MOONLIT MAGIC
ENCHANTED MAGIC
CELESTIAL MAGIC
EVERLASTING MAGIC
CAPTIVATING MAGIC
DISCOVERED MAGIC
LATENT MAGIC

The Thorne Witches: Happily Ever Afters:
ENDURING MAGIC
BOUNDLESS MAGIC

FRACTALED MAGIC

The Unlucky Charms:
<u>*PINTS & POTIONS*</u>
<u>*WHISKEY & WITCHES*</u>
<u>*BEER & BROOMSTICKS*</u>
<u>*COCKTAILS & CAULDRONS*</u>
<u>*WINE & WARLOCKS*</u>
<u>*HIGHBALLS & HEXES*</u>

Sentinels of Magic:
THE AETHER
<u>*THE DEATH DEALER*</u>
<u>*THE SEER*</u>
<u>*THE TRAVELER*</u>
THE SIREN

These Boots Are Made For Witching:
WICKED WITCHMAS
WANTON WITCHMAS

The Angels of Legend:
<u>*LUCIFER*</u>

CONTEMPORARY & ROMANTIC SUSPENSE

Stonebrooke:
<u>*BURNING RESOLUTION*</u>
<u>*HIDDEN RESOLUTION*</u>

The Holt Family:

GOODBYE TO YOU

THIS TIME YOU

INCLUDING YOU

A LIFE WITH YOU

Fiore Vineyard:

PICTURE THIS

RETURN HOME

ONE WISH

BIO & FOLLOW LINKS

T.M. Cromer is a multi-award-winning sorceress of the written word and fearless architect of high-stakes paranormal romance. With a flair for twisty plots, slow burns, and swaggering heroes hot enough to scorch the page, she conjures stories that hook readers and refuse to let go. From her cozy PNW lair, flanked by two Hellhounds and an unholy amount of caffeine ambition, she weaves love, danger, and humor into every page. Whether it's witches, sirens, or magical assassins, her characters never behave, and neither do her stories.

When she's not dreaming up new ways to ruin her characters' lives before crafting their HEA, she's daydreaming about swimming with orcas or cackling over a particularly clever line of dialogue. Come for the magic, stay for the heartbreak, and maybe fall a little too hard for a man who only exists on the page.

Want to stay current on what's happening in T.M. Cromer's world? <u>Subscribe to her newsletter</u> to receive release news and promo alerts.

You can also join her VIP reader group on Facebook to chat with her, participate in polls, and stay up-to-date on what's happening. <u>Become a member today!</u>

FOLLOW T.M. CROMER:

facebook.com/tmcromer
instagram.com/tmcromer
tiktok.com/@tmcromer
pinterest.com/tmcromer
amazon.com/stores/T.M.-Cromer/author/B011QK3WXY